Richard Hill Sandys

Egeus

And other Poems

Richard Hill Sandys

Egeus
And other Poems

ISBN/EAN: 9783337401467

Printed in Europe, USA, Canada, Australia, Japan

Cover: Foto ©Andreas Hilbeck / pixelio.de

More available books at **www.hansebooks.com**

EGEUS

&c.

E G E U S

AND OTHER POEMS

BY

RICHARD HILL SANDYS, M.A.

OF LINCOLN'S INN, BARRISTER-AT-LAW
AUTHOR OF 'IN THE BEGINNING' 'ANTITHEISM' ETC.

LONDON
KEGAN PAUL, TRENCH, & CO., 1 PATERNOSTER SQUARE
1886

CONTENTS.

EGEUS.

Theseus, on parting for Crete on his expedition against Minos, agreed with his father, Egeus, king of Athens, that if successful he would on his return show a white sail as a signal of victory. He did return successful, but forgot to display the promised sign.

On Sunium's height, unhallowed yet by fame
Of glorious deeds, there sat from morn till eve
An aged man, of stately port, whose brow
Serene, and steadfast glance far more than all
Form and appliances of splendid place
Avouched him to be one that never yet
Moved at the bidding of created man ;
When men were all but gods, a king.—But now
From day to day upon the restless wave
That skirts the sea, too soon to bear his name,   10
He looked to where Minoian Cretè lay
Beyond the blue and scattered Cyclades ;
Waiting the triumph of his warrior son,

B

Who without triumph should return no more.

He, at his country's need, in arms had borne

Terms of reprisal and defiance high

To the dread Cretan king, the pirates' scourge,

The mighty ruler of the seas, a shade

In distant councils and a word of fear ;

The breaker up of thrones, the iron rule,   20

Measure for measure, without mercy just.

And now he tarried long, and by degrees

Care and uncertainty and racking dread,

Like wingèd harpies borne by all the winds,

Preyed on the aged father's lonely heart.

Before his eyes the glancing waters broke

Day's universal beam with pleasing change ;

Fair isles in distance softening far away

From point to point to heaven's own proper hue ;

And all his own ; and jutting promontory,   30

And bending coast, and havens half-concealed,

And many a snowy sail and burnished prow

Of argosy and galley that for him

Sped on their courses in the cheerful day.

But now he saw them not :—behind him spread

The land of the olive groves, and arts, and arms,

The eye of Greece, Athenè's throne on earth ;

Where, in the shade of their immortal rock,

The Acropolis, the proud Autochthones,

Created there, nor soiled with duller climes,   40

Walked, delicate in thought, in spirit high,

In form and gesture like the very gods,

And all his own ; but now he had no eyes

Save for his son—sense, thought of joy, except

In some remembered grace of his dear son.

Silent and stern the livelong day he sat ;

And not a shadow on the ruffled wave,

Nor the sad moaning by the idle wind

Made through the bending rushes as it past,

But found true answer in his troubled breast.   50

And if at times his aged servitor,

Of faith long proved, and scarred in the self-same wars,

Should press some gentle service, hopeful word,

Entreaty mild, or loving-kind reproof

For state neglected and too stubborn grief,

Resentful he at first, and all the king,

Would like an angry lion chafe ; but soon

B 2

Resumed his better nature, and conceived

For slight wrong disproportionate remorse,

As in requital, being kindly ever,   60

Turn, faintly smiling, to some gracious tale

Of their own primes, well spent, nor wanting praise ;

But rounding ever with his son—his form,

His grace, his bearing—how he struck the boar,

How he would wind the fiery steed, in all

The exercise of youth how perfect he !

How he reproved the saucy embassy !

And, had he marked, with what fine modesty

He stayed his youthful counsels, nor would take

The applause that sought but welcome, without first 70

The full approval of a father's eye.

He was all spotless ; what to rival him,

Young Œdipus, the glozing boy of Thebes,

Or all the Argonauts and robber sons

Of Tantalus, or, but for the blood of Jove,

His hidden privilege, Alcides' self !

Then would he plan how best to grace his son

When he returned, as sure he would, and soon ;

And how his hunting spears, in order ranged

By his own hands and sacred to his touch,   80

Should rust no more ; and that his faithful dog,

The good Molossian slumbering at his feet,

That at the sound of his young master's name

Lifted intelligent his stately head

To wait his sign, should service take again,

And wake Cithæron with his deep-toned cry ;

That Dian well should deem Orion come,

Lit from the Zodiac—should she not, old friend ?

And he would lay his weary greatness down ;

With his own hands the golden circle place   90

Upon his son's fair brow, and render up

With willing bend, half homage, half caress,

His state, well changed to live awhile in him ;

Then at no distant day, upon the close

Of some new triumph worthily achieved,

Breathe happily his perfect soul away.

So fondly thus the old man garrulous,

Would cheat awhile his sore foreboding thoughts.

But ever and anon, the venomed dart

Struck by the shadowy arm of watchful grief,   100
All keener for his short uneasy rest,
Would reach his quivering soul, and with a start
And stern repulse, for suffering quickens hate,
Drawn to himself, the unhappy king would take
His state once more in wilful loneliness.

Nor needed great occasion then to strike
From his deep sorrow rash unsteady wrath.

' This was their doing—slaves and dastards all·—
Had they no sons? no safety but their fears?
Must he alone live desolate for them,   110
Lutists and revellers, and their effeminate homes?
Theirs was the quarrel—what were they to him?
His sceptre was from Jove, his strength on high ;
And, by the gods ! he was too merciful ;
But he would fling that mercy to the winds,
And teach his thoughts such plagues to vex their
      souls,
That they should deem the Cretan come indeed,
Though he were fitter judge for raging hell.

And he would hold the universal state
But his son's hostage ; look they to themselves.'   120

But now a sail, a snow-white sail, draws on,
Scarce seen at first, but brightening as it comes.
From height to height the joyous signal springs,
From these to rest, but through no weary flight,
Upon the sacred hill ; from that to flash
Its signal to the skies, as thus once more,
To draw new favours by new merits down.
From door to door the busy rumour spreads :
And many a fluttered matron clasps her child ;
And at the fountains many an urn runs o'er,   130
Where maidens stand and smile with downcast eyes,
Lost in sweet fancies, sighing yet not sad,
And blushing deep though not a soul be near.

And Athens wakens to her proper life,
And turns her ever-restless people forth.
Now in her market-place are clasping hands,
Greetings and questionings, and raisèd brows :
Old grudges die ; the peaceful citizen

Sets his cicada with a martial air ;

The warrior grimly smiles, and counts his turn ;   140

No churl so base, that grinds his soul for gain,

But takes some glow of gentle rivalry ;

But all too soon, his hasty chaff burnt out,

Turns with some scurrile jibe of wounds and death,

And sorry feasts, contentment and full sleep,

Back to his villain-craft : the nobler slave

Pants for his freedom now with nearer hope.

The startled minstrels prove their golden lyres ;

The priesthood fret, and on the sacred way

The wreathèd victims, as they feel the god,   150

Turning their curled fronts and gilded horns,

Submissive to the hand, and perfect all,

Pace gently to the very altar's foot.

And on the triumph swells ; each glittering speck

Spread to its full proportions now rides on

A stately galley, every bank complete ;

Fretting with glistening oars the silver tide,

That on its quivering surface still reflects

The glowing pageant as it flies along,

Set in white spray that beams around like stars : 160

Straight to the port they glide ; upon the decks

Stand well-known forms, distinct in order true,

That with their spears upon their dinted shields,

In cadence just, with voices well attuned,

Raise high the pæan note of victory ;

That with her thousands Athens catching up

Sends from her busy shores to all her hills :

So happily they come—but not his son.

'Twas but some idle armament that brought

Spoils and submission from some rebel isle. 170

And now his spirit fell ; and the deep grief

That charms the meaner sense from taste of pain,

O'er the wide gap of his dejected hope,

Rushed on his heart and set its temple there.

No feeling now : the season touched him not ;

He spoke, he heard no more ; and to his side

Drew wandering death, at whose unseen approach

Men fall into strange shudderings, and break off

The tale, and, staring into vacancy, 179

Stand wrapt and listening, though no sound be heard ;

As if a summoning spirit spoke their names

Home to the inner sense ; with sometimes tears

Unbidden, or wild laughter without cause.

So at his side the despot of the world

Stood, and with bony finger proved his dart :

From which dry contact issue fiery pain,

Dread and despondency, and sharp regret—

But healing sure ; rare visions and sweet sounds ;

For heaven opens when a good man dies,

And without voice, nor yet to outward view   190

Vouchsafed, but wakening still in holy dream,

The memories of all clinging charities,

The very forms and graces most endeared

Of the long past, that seem on us to smile,

To charm from earth the weary soul away,

Unnumbered spirits from their seats of bliss

Speed on the untiring ministry of grace

From God to man ; and as the sun's rich beams,

Upon the pathless wood, at glowing noon,

Through yielding boughs or lightly falling leaves,   200

Pierce to some deep neglected solitude,

Some chilly wilderness of damp and shade,

Soon where they light the rugged scene grows mild ;

The air wafts perfume as the tangled sward

Turns by degrees its hidden treasures forth !

From the rude bent with them the lily peeps,

In maiden state the blushing eglantine

Adjusts her soft robe on her briery throne ;

The violet lends its bloom, the thorn its may,

The jasmin softly twines ; all loveliest flowers   210

Spring silent there, forsaken, yet how sweet !

Where without them were rottenness and death. .

So they into the sullen heart of man,

Wooing their welcome ever, so but once

Ill passions, their fell purpose unfulfilled,

Waver an instant, or the stubborn will

Yield but a crevice, fling their living light ;

At which strong charm the angry storm grows
       hushed ;

The heavy mist rolls off and gives to view

An opening paradise of peaceful thoughts.   220

And from their banishment come meekly home,

The graces of the soul : yet one alone,

Her mission sped, for now no future is—

Enchanting Hope flits smilingly away.

But Faith abides, and heavenly Charity,

That bears so rich a charm, that where she comes

Is earth no more, and might she but once place

Her gentle footstep on the sulf'rous plain

Of raging Hell, itself were Hell no more.

O holy Death, feigned hideous by our sins !   230

Thou, that must come, perchance this instant art

To me the dawn of the unsetting day !—

—What if the toll that marks this midnight hour,

Be now my knell, and I must die—alone ?

Yet come not sudden, Death ; nor when success,

Delusive ever, chains more firmly down

The spirit that but seems to mount ; nor when

Defeat and shame in this our pleasant life

Chill the soft current of our delicate joys,

And the permitted fiends that by the side   240

Of sullen outlaws pace with equal steps,

With swift suggestion whisper there unseen,

Of pleasures fled, the wrongs and scorn of those

That, meaner deemed, are yet our very selves ;

And every circumstance of present suffering,

Distorted so by their foul sorceries,

That the smooth stream or bloody grave seems well

To the racked soul a refuge sure, the realm

Of dreamless sleep, and He, the God of all,

Or chance or destiny, or else He rules   250

Careless alone, nor heeds the man He made.

Then come not, Death, for there are but the love

Of life disguised when life's delights are past.

But saving thus, nor tainting thus the soul,

Patient at last and teacher to itself,

Come when and as thou wilt——

Yet is a sorrow sharper far than death,

To higher natures, that, subduing self,

Twine their strong loves in failing age, and live

In younger souls, whose fair succession seems   260

Another life far sweeter than their own ;

Ennobling thus by what embitters most,

When fate untimely strikes ; and therefore he,

Encircled close by sad and watchful friends,

From day to day upon the restless wave

That parted his dear son looked sadly on :

He on the wave, they only upon him.

But still the despot stayed the certain dart,

Which in a tyrant's wantonness he oft

Brandished on high, delaying still to strike.   270

Whilst at each moment fell some prop away.

The royal spirit, nursed in empire, train'd

By heroes that half worshipped as they taught,

Rich in all virtues, practised in high deeds,

To win all hearts beneath his happy rule,

And make subjection seem but privilege

To the proud equals of all kings beside,

Passed with his hope to wander in a world

Of shadows, where one only image now,

In swiftly changing scenes of pain or joy,   280

But seeming all, that through his sickly brain

Rushed like the drift of some wild hurricane,

Stood present ever—yet how far removed !

Now nature gave her signs : the eye that late

Beamed like a star on all the lesser world

Now dim with sluggish tears looked dully round,

Or from beneath its pent of snowy white,

Glared wild and sudden, like the fiery glance

Of some fell monster from its wintry den.

All state declined, all order lost, he now   290

Reeled like a drunken man, or feebly crouched,

Muttering inaudibly with vacant stare

Some idle tale outrunning still his thoughts,

Repeated oft, and all beside himself.

Or he would turn and frame him auguries

From flight of birds or falling leaves, and take

Gladness or sorrow from the natural stir

Of careless life ; or else, forgetting all,

Set him to watch with childlike eagerness

The worthless chances of some idle waif,   300

Helplessly driven by the eddying surge :

Which he would freight with some poor phantasy

Of his sick brain, that being but the shade

Of his past sorrow long indulged, he thus

Would mark, and yearning by degrees, and now

Fairly distracted, take the puny stray

For something undefined, but near his heart ;

And at its wreck, the ready tears would start,

Slow and unnoticed, but through that slight breach,

Anon the bitter tide of his true sorrow   310

Would pour a wintry deluge on his soul,

And he would bend and veil him in his robe,

And weep apart, long, fast, and silently.

Then—for the body that must pine with us,

Has yet its privilege—at length, though but

As one who takes a respite on the rack,

Faintly restored, he slowly would unfold

His anguished brow, and, seeing his true watch

Saddening for him, and being kindly ever,

Take an enforced show of patient hope,   320

That his poor suffering friends afflicted more,

Than all his waywardness and passion past.

And they would turn their manly fronts aside,

One to the other, weeping unrestrained,

Rival on rival leaning, hand in hand.

But on the stranger cast such threatening glance,

As saints on sacrilege, that he should dare

To look upon the ruin of their king.

For they remembered all his gentle rule;

He was to them a god, his eye their star,   330

His strength their peace, sufficing fame his praise;

And there was not among them all one man

Might ever tax him with a wilful wrong,

Or fair endeavour met with curt reproof,

Or biting taunt, that, from the kingly lip

Unanswerable, drives high spirits mad,

And meaner men to dark conspiracy.

And therefore lived his image in their heart,

And when men spoke his name, their thoughts grew
     proud,

And when he ailed, was sorrow round their hearths, 340

Their homes were cold—— And something, too, of
     him,

The lost, the long-desired, for whom they trained

Their gallant boys, whose eyes swept not the ground,

But looked erect and quailed not where they looked,

That met reproof unflinching, though suffused

With silent tears, that fell not to the ground.

These daily now returning from their tasks,

With bounding steps and looks elate, to tell

Their prowess, and their praise how fairly won,

They, happy fathers, with such softness met,   350

And womanly tenderness, as they were fain

Lest they be quite unmanned, to hide beneath

Some show of mirthful taunt, misprising thus,

What gave their mellowed age its dearest charm ;

Which they in turn, detecting quick how true

And deep affection lurked in such disguise,

Would answer in like mood ; and bid them all

Look to their trophies, guard their honours well,

For they would soon o'ertop the chief of all,

And in despite would so acquit themselves,   360

That, by the gods ! when their good prince came back,

He should not choose but lead them to the wars.

And these their youthful chief now wanted long ;

And heavily in grief the days passed on.

But in all time the changeful seasons roll.

And now the autumn wanes ; beneath the shade

The conscious beauties, each supporting each,

Bashful by turns and serious, stand no more

To hear the modest shepherd's artless tale ;

And in the quiet grove, no youthful pair,   370

Pace hand in hand to tell their happy loves

And plan their simple homes, and wonder where

In such fair world should suffering be found,

Whilst often their full hearts deny them words.

Age stirs no more abroad : the twittering flight

Of swallows now makes cheerful eve no more.

The air grows thick, and every sullen gust

Wrenches the brown leaves from their rugged stems,

To scud before the gale, and wavering long,

Sink by degrees, and rest in clammy heaps.　　380

No more the seagull soars on moveless wing

In the soft air upon its lazy watch ;

But, wheeling close and frequent, breasts the spray

With busy scream, and brushes oft the surge ;

Or dips adroit, and flutters on the edge,

Then turns aslant, and, yielding to the gale,

Darts like an arrow and is seen no more.

And seaward, o'er the dull horizon now

Creep heavy mists, that, mounting in thick clouds,

Hang overhead—a fitting canopy　　390

For the last act of some deep tragedy.

And o'er the wintry flood a lonely bark,

That, dimly viewed through clinging vapours damp,

Scarce held the sluggish air, comes slowly on

Floating afar and hardly seen to move ;

That to their dark imaginings seemed well

Some thing of fate, or Charon's dismal raft.

Yet they, for aye the generous and brave,

Are slowly credulous of coming ill,

When they would bind the wreath of honour on,   400

Such thoughts would banish as in scorn.   But he—

He saw it not ; his eye was filmed, his thoughts

Afar, and commune held with sense no more.

And yet he moved uneasily, and flung

With trembling hand his snowy hair aside,

Sighing as one who, in a feverish bed,

Some new delusion takes in troubled dream.

And onward still it came, with wreathless prow,

Blank decks and tarnished sail, and drooping forms,

And every symbol of disastrous flight.   410

For something not quite well—perchance the air

Bore in its liquid void the wailing cry

Of a wronged maiden, ere came wandering by

He, the first tamer of the cruel Ind,

Whose better spirit shared in Northern climes,

Yet lives in chiefs of nations then unborn.

And he, victorious, came as though he fled,

A god was on his track, and in his heart

The heavy thought of an unworthy deed ;

And he forgot the token for his sire,   420

Perplexed thus, or else he did not dare

To claim his triumph when he might not taste

The very triumph he his country brought,

Being such deep subjection in his soul.

And they, beholding now the goodly ship

Themselves had launched so hopeful, thus returned

Assurèd well that he was dead : for how

Should he from Cretè and her bitter king,

The rival of their princes, and the foe

By field and flood of all their land, that held   430

With man no converse, nor regarded aught

The cheerful gods that haunt the hill or grove

Or sedgy stream, or guard the good man's hearth,

The gloomy worshipper of Dis alone,[1]

[1] So Homer, of Achilles,

Οὔτε τέῳ σπένδεσκε θεῶν, ὅτι μὴ Διὶ πατρί.

Sustain defeat and live ?   Dejected thus,

Together in sad concert then they closed

On him their charge, now needing chiefest care,

When aid was none ; whereat the unhappy king,

His vigil ended thus, fell shrieking down,

On the cold ground, there lay as he were dead.   440

But yet he might not die, and yet awhile,

The crimson current flowed, and with it life,

But life in bitterness, life desolate,

Life without purpose, object, aim, each pulse

But a new torment ; sense, intelligence,

Thought, judgment, all in one sharp pang confused.

And thus at last abrupt to his full height,

He wildly leapt, and tore with desperate hands

His snowy locks, untended long, and flung

To the keen air, which, haply borne around   450

By the rude eddy, seemed as brandished there

By viewless hands of Furies on the watch,

In token of their certain victory.

Now reason fled, and he might err no more.

He was a sinless man, whose deadly glance

Scowled hate to man, defiance to the gods,

He that would slay the poor imploring friends,
That but opposed untiring love to rage,
And fain would die might they thus bring him peace;
That bared his bosom to the storm, and clenched 460
His lifted hands, and dared heaven's angry bolt ;
Whose speech was coarsest railing, yells and shrieks
Of aimless vengeance ; he that writhed and strove
In the sad conflict with the kindly force,
That would but guard him from himself ; that foamed,
And bit with bloody jaws the faithful breasts,
That covered hearts that ever beat for him.

Long thus he strove uncertain ; for the loss
Was theirs, and they were old, and wasted long
With the same sorrow that had broken him ; 470
And lessened, too, by awe, that they should thus
With subject hands profane the kingly form.
But now, for with a madman's force there came
A madman's cunning, as content at last
To yield, and tranquil as a child he lay.
Whereat, relaxing by degrees, with joy
For such sweet patience, gladly they resumed

Their old observance, and but sought to calm

With soothing words the reas'ning soul returned.

But at the unguarded moment he at once   480

Broke fiercely from them all, and, laughing wild,

Rushed headlong to the rude and dizzy cliff ;

As men for life, so ran he to his death.

Ah ! had he but beheld that peerless form

Advancing, bounding, flying to his side !

True he had died, but died as age would die.

On to the brink he sped, a moment turned

In desperate glee, then flung him from the height !

And the hushed sea received a senseless form,

Whilst where he had stood, what seemed himself

    restored   490

To brilliant youth, as risen from the ground,

His princely son came on, and all too late !

THE DEATH OF PRIAM.

Æneid, bk. 2, v.

UNHAPPY Priam ! when the deep red blaze
Flashed its sure tidings to his aching gaze
Of falling Ilium, and the hot crimson tide
Through his loved home streamed reeking at his side,
The time-worn warrior o'er his weak limbs hung
His long disused arms, and feebly slung
His pond'rous sword, then, wild and beating high
With life's last fever, faltered forth to die.

Within his palace walls an altar rose,
Uncovered to the sky, where rooted close,   10
An antique laurel, spreading overhead
Its leafy veil, a holy twilight shed
There Hecuba and her sad daughters sought,
Thronged like storm-driven doves, and all distraught,

Aid from their silent gods, and cowering, round

Their imaged forms their weak arms vainly wound.

There, as she saw the aged monarch pass,

Staggering in youthful panoply, ' Alas !

Unhappy husband, what dire fancy charms

Thy thoughts,' she cried, 'to these delusive arms ?   20

The time nor these, nor thee ; not from the grave

Restorèd now my Hector's self should save.

Here, only here ; this altar shall defend,

Or, failing this, one blow one sorrow end.'

So as in age o'ertaxèd nature stays

Her purpose soon, and consciously obeys,

Drawn to her side he took his silent state ;

There, save his wavering eye, as moveless marble sate.

But now the young Polites, his fair son,

From the hot chase in terror pressing on,   30

Through the long halls and lonely columns reels,

Stricken and weak, and Pyrrhus at his heels ;

And now the hunter holds him, now the spear

Finds his white neck, and roots it deeply there.

And onward close before the very eyes,

Of Priam borne, he staggers, falls, and dies.

He, wretched father, then though instant death

Stood in his path, nor passion spared, nor breath;

'Now all the gods, what gods above us,' cried,

'These holiest ties have known, their vengeance

    guide   40

To thy vile heart, and edgeless fall thy sword !

Be cursed thou, for this thy deed abhorred,

That to mine age this foul despite has shown,

And clouds my vision with a slaughtered son !

Not such Achilles, whom, when thou dost lie,

Thou claim'st as thine, to his strong enemy.

He, like a god, the suppliant raised, and gave

The foe that wronged him to a warrior's grave ;

With honoured gifts restored me to my reign,

For this thy shame, that him in me dost stain.'   50

Then threw his cumbrous spear, that, rising slow,

Scarce reached the shield, and fell without a blow.

Then Pyrrhus—' King, thyself the tidings speed,

Hence to the shades of my despitious deed.

There tell thy wrongs, and to Achilles there

Of his degenerate son this token bear ;

Now die ! '—and scarce he ended thus, when o'er

Polites' corse, and sliding in his gore,

He dragged him to the altar's foot, and through

His fluttered heart his reeking weapon drew.   60

So, while for aid his falling country cried,

In burning Troy discrowned Priam died !

And Asia's ruler, the all-powerful lord,

Through many a land in many a tongue adored,

Now lies a headless trunk, a mark for shame,

On the rude shore, a wreck without a name.   66

ACHILLES AT THE TRENCHES.

APPROVED of Jove, Achilles sternly past

Forth from his tent unarmed, yet Pallas cast

Her watchful ægis round, and o'er his head

A golden cloud of dazzling glory spread ;

Alone he stept, nor mingling with the rest,

His promise held, and from his powerful breast

Sent the huge shout which Pallas with her own

Swelled fiercely, whose intolerable tone

Shook all the ranks of Ilium, like the sound

Of the hoarse trumpets when, embattled round   10

Some powerful city, countless host, raise high

The note of onset ; which appalling cry

They the flushed victors sickened when they heard,

And nerveless drooped as back the wild steeds reared

Ungoverned on their cars, or swerved in flight,

And all was rout and measureless affright,

Nor spirit was there one, but quailed

At that fierce form in matchless splendour veiled.

Thrice from the trenches came that sound of dread,

And, feebly rallied, thrice the Trojans fled,   20

Or in the crush fell headlong to the plain,

By their own arms and clashing chariots slain.

So came the welcome evening on at last,

And o'er their flight its timely shadow cast.

Yet scarcely they, for fear removed afar,

Drew rein at last ; and quickly from each car,

Fasting themselves, the panting coursers loosed ;

On straight to council, standing round, confused

And trembling every man, full sorely scared,

Because Achilles had once more appeared.   30

ACHILLES ARMING.

Iliad

THEN, as the snow in winter's gloomy reign
From deep dull clouds falls glittering o'er the plain,
The rallied Greeks rejoicingly once more
Spread from their ships, and whiten all the shore ;
From countless helms the glassy sparkles fly ;
Shields flash on shields, and kindle to the sky,
And laughs the field around with living light,
The busy stir amid, and muster to the fight.
Achilles, all pre-eminent, arrays
For battle in his place ; twin-torches blaze   10
His wrathful eyes, and furiously his breath
Comes hissing forth from his firm grating teeth
In the deep utterance of his vengeful hate
To hapless Troy, and signal of her fate,

So dreadfully in arms he shines again,
In the rich gifts that Vulcan wrought with pain.

NOTE.

Homer has been celebrated for the great variety of his death-giving blows ; but Lucan has, it may be seen, in one instance at least, checkmated him.   He has one of his soldiers hit with javelins in the back and breast at the same instant.   They meet in the middle, and recoil the same way they came.

> ' Terga simul pariter missis et pectora telis
> Transigitur : medio concurrit pectore ferrum ;
> Et stetit incertus flueret quo volnere sanguis :
> Donec utrasque simul largus cruor expulit hastas,
> Divisitque animam, sparsitque in volnera letum.'
>
> *Pharsalia*, l. 3, v. 587.

> ' The sharp points drive at once through back and breast,
> Meet with a clash, and strike fire in his chest.
> The blood, sore puzzled at the double breach,
> Spouts out the life divided, part at each.'

Racine, perhaps from this passage, calls Lucan *Virgile ivre*, the poet evidently seeing double—two spears, two blows, and two spigots.   It requires a little preparation perhaps—

> ' Ut liber animus sentiat vim carminis.'
>
> *Phædrus.*

It reminds one somewhat of the counter-paradox of Queen Elizabeth's waxwork maid of honour—once, I believe, if not still, in Westminster Abbey—who died of the prick of a needle.

On the other hand, Lucan makes Cæsar speak to his
mutinous soldiers as none but Cæsar could speak :

> Discedite castris :
> Tradite nostra viris ignavi signa *Quirites*.
> At paucos, quibus hæc rabies auctoribus arsit,
> Non Cæsar sed pœna tenet : procumbite terræ,
> Infidumque caput, feriendaque tendite colla.
> Et tu, quo solo stabunt jam robore castra,
> Tiro rudis, specta pœnas et disce ferire,
> Disce mori. *Pharsalia*, lib. v. ver. 357.

Begone and clear the camp ; give up to men
My standards, ye faint-hearted *citizens*.
But you, the few from whom arose this rage,
Not Cæsar now, but vengeance, holds : bow down
Your faithless head, and bare your necks for death
Untried recruit, my soldier from this time,
Look on, and learn to strike, to die.

ŒDIPUS.

Statius, Thebaid, bk. 8.

As when the blind and ghastly Œdipus,
Gladdening with presage of that country's fall
Himself had saved, and late so dearly loved,
Strode without guide, unbidden, to the feast
Of his detested son ; there drank to all,
And taxed the lawless rioters as tame
And laggard in their cups upon the eve
Of such fair enterprise—dismay awhile
At that fell grisly shape, Apollo's hate,
To the broad day from his abhorred retreat   10
Arisen thus, held them suspense and mute ;
But soon false shame and forcèd rivalry
Restored them, and their wicked thoughts rushed on
In wilder and yet wilder mirth, as he

Were craven most who least blasphemed—but lo !

The shadow of advancing Nemesis,

The unseen, the unmocked, eternal Nemesis !

At once their stricken senses reel ; their eyes

Dim with unwonted tears ; their laughter drops

To aching sobs ; the spiced air turns forth 20

The reek of the charnel, and the sparkling wine

Dulls and ferments to noisome must, and thus

In speechless consternation staring wild,

They gnash their teeth despairingly, and champ

Their dainty viands, fouled with blasts from hell,

That work a loathing e'en more terrible

Than all the torments of the morrow's death. 27

LABERIUS.

Laberius, a Roman knight, a man of some genius, and celebrated as a writer of mimes, being compelled to appear on the
stage by the request of Julius Cæsar, the step involving the loss
of his knighthood, is said to have spoken the prologue here
translated from Macrobius.

NECESSITY ! against whose crooked tide

So many strive that ever strive in vain !

Where hast thou borne me thus defenceless forth,

In the extreme of this my wearied age ?

Me no ambition, me no rivalry,

No strife, no fear, strength, or authority

From honour's path e'er turned in glowing youth.

Yet see, in age how princely excellence,

Affably speaking in persuasive tones,

Moves without effort from my place of rest !   10

For man must yield where not the gods withstand,

And I this morn, full thirty years twice told,

And all without a stain, that left my home

A Roman knight, must now return a player !

And I by this one day have lived too long.

Yet if it were, indeed, thy purpose thus

For lettered praise to break off the chief flower

Of my good fame, O ! potent Nature why,

In good and ill alike predominant,

Did'st thou not rather bend the pliant bough   20

In my sweet spring of life? so might I give

Content to these, and win e'en his applause.

But wherefore now ? what bring I to the scene ?

What grace of form, or state, or dignity,

Gesture or bearing, or melodious voice ?

E'en as the cold and clinging ivy kills

The stately oak, so sure does creeping age

Kill me, and I now, like a sepulchre,

Bear nothing but a title and a name.   29

But Laberius took a speedy revenge, and Cæsar could not
have very greatly enjoyed his performance. At his first en-
trance, rushing on the stage in the dress and character of a
slave who had just been severely flogged, his first words (under-
stood to have been introduced by himself) were, ' Porro Quirites

libertatem perdimus.' A little further on he added, 'He must needs fear many whom many fear;' and on another occasion:

> Not through all time is man pre-eminent.
> Reach you the height, uneasily you stand;
> Descend one step, you fall—and I have fallen;
> And soon shall he that follows.   Praise is free.

It may be added that the word *Quirites* above quoted is not very translatable. As the old name for the Roman people collectively, they were somewhat proud of it, and there was a sort of national feeling about it, much as there is about our 'Rule Britannia,' 'Old England,' 'Wooden Walls,' 'thin red line,' and so on, or such as our American cousins attach to their everlasting and ubiquitous 'Stripes and Stars.'

> Τὸ ῥαβδοειδόσημα,
> Τὸ ἀστερόεν φόρημα,
> Κατὰ γᾶν δι' ἁλμυρᾶς τε
> Ἔτι ὕπατον ποτᾶται.

In the quotation from Lucan above given the matter is reversed, as it was there assumed to be a far greater distinction to be a soldier of Cæsar than a mere Roman citizen or civilian.

THE THREE HOROLOGES.

(From the Italian.)

SHADE, wheel, and sand : by line, by steel, by fall,
Dark, hard, minute, slow-moving waste the day.
O deadly shade, that wrapp'st me in thy pall !
O cruel wheel, that drawest my life away !
O heavy sand, to all that live in woe !
With griefs, racks, burthens, do ye hold your sway.
Ye threefold death, gloom, torture, ceaseless flow !
Snares, pains and dangers, aye, o'er life ye spread ;
Dull type of horror, shade to all below !
Blind wheel, that ever urgest as I go !   10
And thou, small dust, mute token from the dead !

LINES

SMILE, little child, on him scarce more than child,
Whose charge, whose thought, whose life thou art :
   look full
Into his loving eyes ; give light to light,
Set gladness free, make patient longing joy,
Enriching take ; so, palm to palm, the touch
Is holy ; from that innocent kiss there sprang
A spirit to the heart, that there enthroned
Shall keep your age not wholly desolate.
Now dash those tears aside, that but set off
Joy quick returning, as this summer breeze   10
Flings from the glossy leaves the genial rain
To glitter in the sun, new broken forth
From sullen clouds, that darts his rich beams o'er

The slanting shower in full retreat, and sets
His radiant arch of triumph in the skies.
Now, side by side, clasp well that faithful hand,
And with dilated eyes and serious brow,
As on a well-concerted enterprise,
Plant firm that little heel ; a brother's care
Shall make those flints as velvet to your tread ;   20
And now, the ravine past, toss back those curls,
And laugh and crow with such sweet merriment
Shall charm the heavy thoughts of broken men,
Sober the midday drunkard, and draw forth
A faltering blessing from regretful age.
Twin treasures, home : your places vacant long
Make gloom, and thoughts sent forth from yearning
      hearts,
Like scouts unseen, are hovering round your path :
Your angels watch for you ; for you this hour
Is joy in heaven—what, also, if for me,   30
Who soften thus at what myself have been,
And take, unmarked of you, a kindred peace,
That, of myself, such peace can never know ?

Eheu ! gymnasii mei sodales

Impubes ! decus, heu, meum, quibuscum

Festive toties novis in armis,

Pro palmâ pueris puer movebam

Lites innocuas citâ palæstrâ !

Ergo fœdere par pari obligati

Dulci, nec superis inauspicatis,

Carpebamus iter periculosum,

Visuri propius scelus, rapinas,

Funestasque acies, atroxque regnum   10

Vitai sua jura vindicantis.

Nunc surda omnia, nec tenent fluenta

Cursus sacra suos ; nihil calet cor !

Sævit luctibus omne sæculum, ipse

Vel somnus furor, et torus sepulcrum.

A MORNING WALK.

(Not after Cowper.)

MARK, where the gallant Minyæ guide
Their Argo o'er the Euxine tide !
A shade at noon—athwart the sky
A stately eagle soars, so high
He parts the light rack's fleecy veil,
So huge his pinions fan their sail.[1]
With one harsh scream the bird of Jove
Unbending cuts his way above,
Then, in the distance sweeping o'er
Black Caucasus, is seen no more.   10
Anon a shriek : from every part,
No warning, seems at once to start.

[1] Νεφέων σχεδόν, ἀλλὰ καὶ ἔμπης
Λαίφεα πάντ' ἐτίναξε παραιθύξας πτερύγεσσι.
APOLL. RHOD. *Argonaut.* bk. ii. v. 1254.

From sea and sky, above, around,
One savage, wild, unearthly sound :
A shrill and miserable cry,
The Titan in his agony !
Where in a hollow far beyond
The springs of life, sweet nature's bound
Hid in the gloomy crags, beneath
The summer's blaze, the winter's breath,   20
Prometheus on his bed of stone
Lies chained, and visitor has none
Save that fell bird, that comes to tear
From his torn side his daily fare.
Down fall the clashing oars, that may
Take equal stroke no more that day.
No warrior there but hides his brow,
Shuddering apart, and crouching low
E'en where he sits ; and not a word,
Or sign, or sound of life is heard   30
Save but at times the gasping sound
Of pain concealed, or look around
Save a quick glance thrown hurriedly
To catch some stronger comrade's eye.

So dread a thing the witnessing,
A higher nature's suffering !
Again at eve the eagle came,
Returned, his flight, his scream the same.
He passed ; and mark ! one bloody speck
From his hot beak now stains their deck.   40

They on their paths : and many an age
Has fled since then, and many a stage
The unwearied car of day has run,
That shines on us as then it shone.
Nations have risen and have set
Since then, and many a name been great.
But Nature varies not : the sea
Rolls on, the pleasant air is free,
And beauteous earth ; the arched groves
Shelter as then our whispered loves,   50
And the broad day surveys the stream
Of thought, life, passion still the same.
Succession without change, and we
Are, and perforce shall ever be,

Their kindred still ; and for that cause

Sweet Nature gently round us draws

A golden chain, unseen by man,

Unbroken since the world began ;

And the great names of early days

Are household words with us : their praise

Fires yet, and kindles in our eyes,

And lifts us with them to the skies.

And I have gentler thoughts this hour,

The bitter day, my night, is o'er.

They sleep that once were mine, and I

Wander alone in phantasy,

That use makes now my life ; my chain

Is off, I am a child again :

As once, when in the morning grey,

In leaden sleep my schoolmates lay,   70

With stealthy touch the bolt withdrawn,

I slipt to greet the golden dawn,

Then o'er the barrier ; turned awhile,

With clenched fist and mocking smile,

To mark my infant triumph o'er

The prison that I hated sore.

Thence pausing soon to note the light
Of the last watcher of the night
When I upon its lessening rays
Would with such childish longing gaze,   80
As I by that might fix it there
In the unstable, faithless air,
Fair star, that when the landscape grey
Takes largesse of usurping day !
And hill, and dale, and tufted lawn
Spread their fresh carpets to the dawn,
Seizing each moment as it flies
New graces from the blushing skies ;
And the dull swamps and fallows brown
Prank them in colours not their own ;   90
And the dark stately groves that through
The peaceful hours, on service true,
Drooping their leafy plumes, have stood
At watch upon the silent flood ;
So calm, so still, the starry beam
That sinks beneath the quiet stream,
Looks back upon the lonely night,
With such a sweet and constant light

As we might deem the glances pure
Of wistful Naiad set to lure   100
Some favoured sister to her side
Beneath the cool translucent tide :
Soon as the first keen morning air
Shall but the trembling aspen stir ;
Nor yet the glow-worm's light shall fail,
Nor, weakly fledged, the twilight pale
Fall from the hill's defending brow,
Entangled in the mist below ;
Ah ! for true faith ! the whispering breath
That glides the drowsy leaves beneath,   110
Seems as it speaks some charm that draws
The faltering lieges to its cause ;
That, as in concert, straight lay down
Upon the sward their mantles brown,
And in all richest colours vie
In the advancing pageantry ;
Sprinkling rich pearls and odours rare
Upon their sweeter kindred near—
The lowly flowers that love the mead,
Or in the hedgerow lie half hid,   120

Or to the lattice climb, and peep

Where village beauties lie asleep.

While through the groves from every part,

From out the rustling arras start,

With busy chirp, in tabards gay,

The feathered pursuivants of day ;

And as they strain their tawny throats

To spread abroad their wild wood notes,

Wing round a short and restless flight

With such importunate delight   130

As if before in any clime

Were never known such gracious time.

But she, as vowed on mission high,

Stays not to taste of revelry ;

But, like a tempted saint, from all

The gaudy stir and festive call

Passes to seek a purer day

Meekly and silently away.

My worship told—away alone,

A sleeping world is all my own.   140

There's not a sound, or stir, or aught
Of life to chide my truant thought.
The simple dwellings, cold and grey,
That line on either side my way,
To me an eastern city stand,
Unpeopled by some genie's wand :
Such as the lion-hearted bride
Told of a thousand nights, beside
The gloomy Caliph simply won
To hear the tale so well begun.   150
Quick with new life my senses grow.
A fancy hangs on every bough.
The pollard in the twilight dim
Glares on me like an afrite grim.
All things are magical ; that owl
A vizier once, that post a ghoul.

First to the bridge, that tunnelled heap
Of stone ; upon the causey steep,
Above sore creeks the toiling wain ;
Below the waters chafe in vain ;   160

Which though it bear of art no trace,

Yet wins from time a kindly grace.

The olden time ; the idle youth

That graved for fame those lines uncouth,

Sleeps well beneath yon distant stone,

By moss and lichen long o'ergrown.

Where the rank nettle's sickly bloom

Waves slow o'er his forgotten tomb.

Lightly to the forbidden seat,

Outside the crumbling parapet.　　　　170

Through the main arch a Stygian flood

Rolls slow but strong its liquid mud,

Beside the dark and noisome ledge,

Far skirted by the splashy sedge ;

That bounds the quick unsteady sand,

Nor water quite, nor perfect land ;

That seeming firm, is but a cave

Of hollow death, the wanderer's grave.

Oft in the gusty night there comes,

Uncertain to the scattered homes,　　　　180

That with their ruddy lights, disposed

Unequal, and by turns disclosed,

With thoughts of rest and peace beguile,

The weary traveller's lonely toil ;

From the broad waste, a distant cry,

But comes so faint and doubtfully

That the uneasy thought is gone

Unspoken ere it can put on

The airy shape of aught of ill,

The fireside tale and mirth to chill,   190

The morrow dawns ; on all the face

Of earth is not a single trace,

Nor shall be till the end, to tell

How fierce the throes of him who fell,

Heard, but unmarked, that lies below

Tombed in that smooth and deadly slough ;

But far away is doubt and pain,

And sickening hope that clings in vain,

And deep determined grief, that o'er

The threshold *one* returns no more.   200

And the broad sweeping tide, I view

Delighted, has its trophies too.

When autumn thick with vapours drear

Brings up in storms the closing year,

And the wide wastes of water seem,

All bounds confused, no more a stream,

But hid in mists and settling free

On well-known haunts a shoreless sea :

Ah ! the sweet lips that yesternight,

Spoke hope, and joy, and gay delight,   210

When that the gloomy ebb shall fling,

Yon senseless, shapeless, slimy thing,

Upon the swilled and sluggish plain,

Shall never part to smile again.

THE STROLLERS.

(From Crabbe.)

En quîs imperium deest tyranni !
Heroes, sed et impudica turba !
En plebis proceres jugum ferentes
Turpes post operas superbientis !
En lauti qui simul famelicique !
Belli sordiduli, macræque bellæ !
Ipsiusque Helenæ æmulæ puellæ
Solaris facis indicem timentes !
Quarum, utcunque tenent, cavent amantes,
Fucata oscula, scloppio doloso.   10
En victûs inopes graves patroni !
Terrarum domini en levi susurro
Ob stipendia molliter querentes !
Quos tollit populus, premit, regitque !
Qui lentam dominam colunt Vacunam
Infamem sibi vindicantque famam.   16

PALINODIUM

(Not from Crabbe.)

EHEU Thespidis essedariorum
Longâ progenies subacta curâ !
Vobis militia est acerba, vobis
Sunt stipendia tristia emerenda.
Vos poscunt joca, vos modos canoros,
Concinnæque acies vagas choreæ ;
Fastus deinde togæ, trucisque belli
Ardentes gladios, tubas, triumphos,
Mortalesque rogos vicesque rerum ;
Offensæ cupidi, ac fero tumentes   10
Bile ad perniciem expedita turba ;
Tirones male feriati, avari
Obscænique senes, et e popinis
Nattarum omne genus, forique sordes ;
Et qui funereo nitent amomo,
Crudeles oculi potentiorum.

Vos, si forte gravet, quod aut moretur

Fabellæ series, modus laboret,

Aut verbum cadat unicum invenuste,

Gestu atque ore truces, furore cæco,   20

Spe fractos, studio atque mente totâ,

Ad triste exagitant simul cubile.

Matutina tenet recocta crambe ;

Explosi perimunt minæ magistri ;

Urit cura phrenetici poetæ ;

Vespertinus agit timor recenti

Læsos naufragio, severius quod

Regales habitus tegant egenos,

Angat frons hilarisque re dolentes.

Successus, sit, alat, maligna sæpe   30

Fors tantum dedit hoc, brevi potitis

Vobis laude placere non amari.

Sed vos me excipitis labore fessum,

Ægrum casibus, hospites, silentem,

Ex voto faciles, et arte blandâ ac

Totis deliciis gravis Camœnæ,

Lenes pectore suscitatis ignes.

Vobiscum ut spatier vices in omnes

Per sylvestria nunc vagus vireta,

Vocale exilium, sales et inter   40

Lautas tristitias merosque amores :

Tum vernæ peracuta sannionis

Mordacis joca formulasque rixæ.

Horrescam penitus senisve diras

Cadmeias patris in suas furentis ;

Quis presens nimis audiensque numen

Spargit funera dexterâ rubenti.

Nunc ipsis oculis minantis aras

Cernam sanguine Cæsaris madentes,

Juratasque acies fidemque Bruti.   50

Nunc sævum reditum ac manum rebellem

Convivæ Aufidii, stolasque matrum.

Sistam nunc Venetis, ad insolentis

Veronæ modo fana luctuosa.

Ergo Thespidis essedariorum,

Vobis, progenies subacta curâ,

Sint fausta omnia ; sint dies amœni,

Sint sanctique lares, quiesque fessis,

Fautoremque adhibete, meque amicum.   59

THE ALMSMAN.

BLANEY, AN ELDERLY BROKEN-DOWN RAKE, PLACED IN A
CHARITABLE INSTITUTION BY AN ABUSE OF PATRONAGE.

(*From Crabbe.*)

ISTUM videte, quæso, procerum, macrum,
  Semperque pallentem senem !
Quisnamne in illo mille libro abscondita
  Scelera, pavores non legat ?
In ore luctus quantus, et luctu simul
  Amarior festivitas !
Grassantur intus fœda cuncta, sed deest
  Externus haud quidam decor.
Ut triste votum distrahit præcordia,
  Moerorque voto sævior !   10
Ut vultus intranquillus, ut mutat vices
  Ut omnis exulat quies !
Moresne, facies ista non sontem notant
  Anguisque reptantis dolos ?

Attende risum ! rapere sic plausum juvat,
    Obscæna dum effutit joca.
Ignava turba dum probet, quid aut pati
    Aut facere non noster velit ?
Quaterna lustra hunc post peracta proximum
    Excepit e custodibus,   20
Juvenem, beatum, sed nec invenustum ; idem
    Prorsus reliquit perditum.
Vulgare totum est ; trita jam fabellula ;
    Flagitia ne quæsiveris.
Profusus, appetensque, comiter nihil
    Non arrogans vixit sibi.
Tum flos juventæ, spolia opima, ut assolet,
    Viduam, beatamque arripit.
Hinc liber animus, igne ceu tactus seges,
    Exarsit omnis protinus,   30
Assecla cantatricis hic notissimæ,
    Idem hic agasonum comes
Cui nempe in omni sorte conjunctissimus
    Auriga quidam publicus.

Securus omnis ille famæ, et sumptuum
    Oblitus, impotens sui,

Largitor incassum, rependens nemini,
    Facilis, amansque nullius.
Hunc in sacratas hasce sedes incolam,
    Patricius immisit favor.   40
Ut sera vitæ computet dispendia,
    Discatque seclusus mori.

THE DANAIDE.

(From Horace.)

O MERCURY ! through thee by song
  Amphion raised his walls ;
And thine the lyre that wakes the soul
  To joy in festive halls.

Through thee the fiercest beasts grow tame,
  And crouch in pleasure low ;
And woods have moved, and swiftest streams
  Have lingered in their flow.

The savage Cerberus on thee
  Fawns at the gates of Hell ;
The tangled pests that guard his mane
  Unwind them at thy spell.

And in thick sobs, delightedly,
    His dreadful breath he draws ;
The bloody slaver then alone
    Falls harmless from his jaws.

The gloomy giants' iron cheeks
    First soften to a smile ;
The Danaides leave their fatal urns,
    Permitted for a while,

For there the crimes that walk the earth
    Their late requital gain ;
And they in ceaseless anguish there
    Sore rue their husbands slain.

Of fifty brides that night but one
    The deadly mandate stayed
One gentle spirit, nobly false
    Her perjured sire betrayed.

'Wake, dearest,' as her youthful lord
  Lay hushed in soft repose,
She whispered soft ; ' beware the sleep
  That no awakening knows.

.⚡

'Speed from these halls of death : around
  My father sets his snare ;
Fierce as she-wolves, their helpless prey
  My cruel sisters tear.

'Of all your kin not one again
  The light of day may see ;
I only keep my hand unstained—
  I could not injure thee.

' And let my father bind these limbs
  In adamantine chain,
Or place me where sweet pity's voice,
  May ne'er be heard again.

‘ But speed you, dearest husband, while
    Yet night and love may save ;
And o’er the tomb of my true love
    The plaintive record grave.’

CONTRIBUTIONS.

LINES ON THE DEATH OF THE PRINCE IMPERIAL.

June 1, 1879.

The disaster at Isandlana, redeemed by the saving of the colours, drew the young Prince out to Zululand. A small cross which he wore (the gift, it is said, of Pope Pius IX.) was re-garded with such superstitious awe by the savages on stripping the dead body, that they forebore to take it away.

TEARS dimmed the mother's loving glance,
    When glowing with Ambition's fire
She saw th' Imperial Child of France
    Kneel by the ashes of his sire.

The sword refused by France, that asked
    No service at her exile's hand,
He girded for the war that tasked
    The sinews of his foster-land ;

F

Whose standard, with th' heroic blood
Of Melvill and of Coghill stained,
Rose weeping from the sheltering flood,
By hands of foemen unprofaned.

He thought to grace th' Imperial name
With laurels gathered in the van,
And upon distant fields reclaim
The sceptre broken at Sedan.

—Surrounding a dismounted troop,
Peer from their ambush in the reeds
Fierce, night-black faces, whose war-whoop
Strikes sudden spurs in startled steeds.

With broken saddle-girth, one horse,
Without his rider rushing by,
Has left by yon lone watercourse
A prince to battle and to die.

With ruthless hands, that spared but one
—One—holy gift, the robbers tore
The splendours from their prey, whose sun
Went down in blood for evermore.

That cross, whose mute appeals rebuke
The thoughts that dwell on sceptred sway,
Shot forth a secret power that shook
The foes who stript his bleeding clay. .

Again beside his sire's remains
The young Marcellus rests his head ;
And the all-lonely Empress reigns
Supreme in sorrow o'er her dead.

JOHN STAFFORD SPENCER.

RELICS.

I.

A HUMAN form, that fifty years had slept
In watery depths, was found within the mines,
The hidden virtues of whose flood had kept
The young face fresh, and marbled its fair lines.
—An aged woman comes, whose heart divines
What thing has risen from that iron gloom
Adown whose void the miner's lantern shines ;
And sees the lover of her youth, whose tomb
Has thus restored his face in all but living bloom.

II.

What vistas opened, as her withered face,
With trouble lined and ripple-marked with tears,

Hung on those features, called from earth's embrace
And all unsullied with the flight of years !
Surely in this the hand divine appears !
Lonely and poor, she knows no other stay ;
Leaning on That, her journey's end she nears,
Soothed by the thought of sleeping with the clay
Raised from the sunless stream, that bore her hopes
    away.

III.

Not such the relics to the king displayed
Who peered within an old imperial tomb,
And viewed the pomp and glittering masquerade
That mocked the dreary vault's sepulchral gloom.
Clad in the richest labours of the loom,
Crown'd, sceptred, seated on a marble throne,
One bony hand amid the musty fume
Laid on his sword ; upon the Gospels, one ;
Was seen the bygone king—a grinning skeleton ! [1]

[1] Charlemagne, whose tomb at Aix-la-Chapelle was visited
by Otho III. of Germany.

JOHN STAFFORD SPENCER.

RIVER VIEWS.

I.

A WANDERER by the river's devious marge,
Whose reeds are stirred by eve's prelusive gale,
I mark the gliding topmast of the barge
That slowly rounds the point with stooping sail,
To pass beneath the bridge with answering hail ;
The flight of martins round the gray church tower,
With bars of sable crost, and ivy's trail ;
The chimes that lend a passion to the hour,
While home the hoppers throng from many a tassell'd
    bower.

II.

Here, where the stream is shaded by deep woods,
A boat lies moored before a gipsy fire :

Now whirring from their leafy solitudes

With soon-lost twitterings, break the feathered choir

Away to hedgerow, battlement and spire :

The fuel-gatherers of their arms despoil,

The bending boughs, to feed the crackling pyre,

That mocks the laughing fanner's smoky toil,

Till, full of fiery tongues, it scars the root-bound soil.

III.

Below the falls, to which the sunset lends

The purple hues that come in evening's train,

Its tidal force the rippling river ends ;

Ebbing and flowing through the rural reign,

And wafting barges to and from the main,

Whose far-off azure rim and softened lines

Of marshy shore, as spied from yon hill chain,

Give place at nightfall to the rolling signs

Shown by the beacon light, that o'er a sandbank shines.

JOHN STAFFORD SPENCER.

SEA VIEWS.

I.

A CHALKY path descends with many a break
Close on the beach, the children's Wonderland,
Who laugh to see the porpoise in the wake
Of curtseying sails ; or, raked up from the strand,
The baby crab, ere through the clawed wet sand
It sinks, self-buried ; or the mussel'd rock,
Part-covered by the tide—a slippery stand—
Now black, now whitened with the billowing shock ;
Or seagulls that with screams to fish-drest pastures
flock.

II.

Now while his mates are hauling in the nets,
Or tossing in the well the scaly spoil,

His vessel's head to shore the fisher sets,

Till, lowering sail, she grounds amid the boil :

The creaking windlass turns the thickening coil ;

Slow creeps the stern above the billow's reach ;

The silver-gleaming produce of their toil,

Like strips of sky, is showered upon the beach

Before the fishwives, whom the seagulls scarce out-
screech.

III.

Oft at low tide the fisher's wife is fain

To send her infants far along the shore

To gather bedded cockles, and sustain

—Till father's boat comes home—her sinking store.

Bare-legged and crimson'd, on from door to door

The baby merchants, ere to school they creep,

The basket hoist, which home with joy they bore

Last evening, when far out had gone the deep ;

But buyers have been few, and they with hunger weep.

JOHN STAFFORD SPENCER.

THE COASTGUARD STATION.

I.

An old rude-shapen stairway up the cliff,
That, haply born of wreckage from the deep,
Stands on the shingle, where a long blue skiff
Lies high and dry above the billow's sweep ;
A flag-staff, whose trim rigging crowns the steep,
And hums and vibrates in the cheerful gales,
Tell where the coastguard their bleak station keep.
—Lines, wet blue flannels, mended oars and sails,
In cottage gardens peep above the tarry pales.

II.

The pebbles, moving with the tide, imbrown
The flowing waters, as they rake the sand

And, ebbing, draw the weed-strewn shingle down.

The lone coastguardsman, telescope in hand,

Whose practised eye the weather-signs has scann'd

And cabled ships sheet-anchoring for the night,

Hears nought but boding cries, as tow'rd the land

The clamorous sea-fowl stretch their necks in flight,

Skimming from buoy to buoy, as sinks the fiery light.

III.

One, whose breast-medal tells of many a life

Plucked by his daring from the billow's roar,

Laughs, while beholding with his busy wife

Their children's play upon the cottage floor,

Where they, trick'd out as rescuers on the shore,

Haul an old rocket-line from hand to hand ;

Till, turned to some new frolic, they implore

A swing by father on the hard wet sand,

Betwixt two boats that lie sun-blistered on the strand.

IV.

Here, knee-deep in the surf, the shrimper wades,

Dipping his net beneath the broken flow

Of waves whereon the rose of sunset fades ;

Till Evening bids the distant beacon show

Faint glimmerings, trembling through the afterglow :

'Mid the long ripples o'er the sandy floor

He ploughs along, with creeping step and slow ;

Or answering one who hails him from the shore,

He heaves his dripping net, then buries it once more.

JOHN STAFFORD SPENCER.

SKETCHES.

I.

WITH thoughts that grow like clusters on the vines
He swells the vintage of his native.tongue,
Claiming all nature in melodious lines—
The glittering dew-drops by the shepherd flung
From the green vine in which his crook is hung ;
The nods and twitterings from the cottage-eaves
Of the house-martins and their callow young ;
Or in the year's decline the wayside leaves
Caught by the harvest-wain, and tangled in the
    sheaves :

II.

The signs of nature : sheep, not softly laid
About the meadow in the morning haze,
But huddled in the corner elm-tree's shade,
Which to the shepherd's skilful eye betrays

The coming on of broken summer days:[1]
The fisher, who amid the Baltic's roar
Quick-rising plates of bottom-ice surveys,
And hastens, ere a firm-cemented floor
Has fixed his idle keel, to set his sail for shore:

III.

The waves at sunset shoaling on the bar
At th' harbour-mouth ; the weather-beaten rowers
Towing to boat-strewn shores a broken spar ;
The anchored frigate, straining at her bowers,
Whose sun-gilt chains the greenish water scours
From floating sea-weeds, which, a moment caught,
Ride the strong ebb that tries her cable's powers ;
Then twilight, when the echoing gun's report
Wakes the low roll of drums within the distant fort.

[1] An old shepherd, on a farm in East Kent, drew my attention
to his flock as we crossed the meadows in the gray dawn :
' Look at my sheep, how well abed they are this morning—a
sure sign of a fine day.   On the approach of unsettled weather,
they will close up under a tree in a corner of the field, even
before a change of sky is seen.'

J. S. S.

IV.

The thoughts of truth and beauty, which his soul
Delivers clear as wines 'upon the lees,'
Are in their first conception as the roll
Of rain-discoloured, sunshine-dappled seas—
The rainbow's floor !—or sea-anemones
Kissed into colour by the tide, and set
In instant motion by the first spray-breeze ;
Their colours fading with the tide's retreat,
Whose ripples, step by step, the furrowed sands repeat.

V.

Swayed as the bell-buoy o'er a dangerous shoal,
That sends from wave to wave a church-like chime,
The poet, as great thoughts break o'er his soul,
Lets fall upon the perilous sea of Time,
And sends from heart to heart, his stirring rhyme.
—With Truth's strong windlass he from Wrong can win
Men's minds, like anchors foul with weed and slime,
Lightly as sailors dance their cable in,
With pleasant choral cheer or merry violin.

JOHN STAFFORD SPENCER.

THE BREAK OF GAUGE.

Κνισμοῦ μὲν ἐκ τοῦδ' ἀντιχείροιν, ὡς δοκεῖ,
Φαῦλόν τι καὶ πονηρὸν ὧδ' εἰσέρχεται.

By the pricking of my thumbs,
Something wicked this way comes.

Μῦς ὅδε ὡρολόγειον ἐφήλατο κύδεϊ γαίων·
Τοῦτο τορῶς ἔβραχ' Ἐν—καῦθις ὅγ' ἂψ' ἔδοαμεν.

DULCE DOMUM.

THE SCHOOLBOY AT HOME.

THE pony's lamed, the cat is dead,

The pigs are in the tulip-bed ;

The flue with rubbish has been filled,

And all my lady's plants are killed ;

A strange wet cur of low degree

Sits dripping on the rich settee ;

The grave mackaw has lost his tail,

And slowly tears a Mechlin veil ;

The pistol's cleaned with sister's shawl

For midday practice in the hall ;   10

The maids are whimpering with affright,

Because a ghost was seen last night ;

The linen's scorched, the roller's split ;

The tangled chain won't turn the spit ;

G 2

The ale is running all about,
And in the urn's a ragged clout ;
And all around at every pass
Is smash and clash and broken glass ;—
And here's a neighbour come to fret,
And, mercy ! there's a hive upset !   20

⁕

AN INVOCATION.

QUEEN of all hearts ! throughout this vexed earth,
Save only when thou payest to scoffing Death
His tributary tale of human lives,
Supreme !   O thou that tak'st thy place anon
In Elfinland with proud Lucifera
And her swart councillors, thyself unseen !
Thou, that in triumph once, the senses' sovereign,
Rod'st with Kehama into Padalon
Through all its gates at once ! that tak'st thy state
High on a car framed of pernicious yew   10
Unseasonably cut in dim eclipse,
When the blue meteor leaped and mandrake shrieked,
In robe of changeful hue, that seems at times
Imperial purple rich with glittering gems,
At times a beggar's rag !—— upon thy brow

Sits high disdain, forethought severe, and what,

Save for that hasty glance and hissing breath,

Drawn inwardly through pale and quivering lips,

Might well be deemed true wisdom self-possessed.

O mock Serenity, thou only falsehood   20

Of noble natures, how dost thou afflict us !

   Before thy feet sits Grief, all ashy pale,

Horribly squalid, rocking to and fro,

Then stubborn most when healing most is nigh

That waits on all ; beside her angry Pain

Impatient stoops, and gnaws his cankered lip

Foul with distempered oozings ; in his hand

A venom-streakèd dart he bears wherewith

At times he strikes exultingly, and speeds,

Racked but impenitent, some thriftless soul   30

Upon the dread unknown——

                         Yet now beneath thy glance,

Dwarfed to a very Aztec, pines away,

Resentful of his power retrenched by thee.

   And ever at thy chair an Antic stands,

Who, lean and haggard, shakes his bauble tipped

With hissing snakes, while o'er his pallid cheek

Convulsions ever flitting tell the tale

Of conscious shame and undivulgèd dread ;

And thus, lewd hireling, looks he round for sight

Of pain or abject wretchedness which he   40

May aptly turn to sŏme keen biting jest

To waken laughter in thy musing court.

    Thee on thy passage trail a sacred team

Of chosen steeds, o'erweighted with themselves ;

Uncomfortable, slow as Stygian flood,

Misers of speed and whipping-stocks of gibes ;

That mope with drooping heads and unchamped bits,

Or, if they move, resentful of the wrong,

Scarce step by step their heavy feet transplant,

To root anew at every weary stamp.   50

These bear thee on through all this pleasant earth,

Their flowery path, which as they pass they cloud

With brooding fogs and exhalations dire,

Wherein no thing or sign of life is seen,

Save through the chilly mist some splashing rat

Or damp uneasy toad ; all flowers grow pale

As weeds of cellar growth ; the fountain pure,

That rears its stainless column, self-adorned

With glittering diamonds, whose tinkling fall

Charms like a fairy spell, at thy approach   60

Drops with a sullen splash, and all is o'er.

Slow is thy state ; yet swifter thou in truth

Than ever arrow shot from Parthian bow,

And freer than the bolt of heaven, and as

The crouching pard upon the fearful hind

Or agile springbok from its covert leaps,

And fastens—aye, full vainly do they bound,

Vainly they fly that with them carry death.

So thou on human thoughts ; and therefore now,

Great Goddess, Mighty Mother, hear me now—   70

Me thy true liege, thy serf and worshipper

From very boyhood—me, this livelong night,

Raving and tossing on my bed of pain :

Come in thy terrors, oh ! if ever, now,

Come, mighty Care—and kill that squalling cat.   75

A CHARADE.

WE rule the world, we letters five,
And thus we sing, and thus we strive.

The crowned king, the belted knight,
 The churl of low degree,
The priest, the statesman, and the thief,
 Are ruled by letters three.

The League and Charter, Church and State,
 And all we say and do,
And little plots and great debates,
 Are ruled by letters two.

From heaven's rich vault of softest blue,
 In showers of roses we ;
And caught their colours as we came,
 Did we the letters three.

Olympian Jove in high divan,
 He split his head half through,
And the bright goddess sprang to life
 That loves the letters two.

When lightly glides the gondolet
 Across the moonlit sea,
Each master-spirit of the earth
 Is ruled by letters three.

They wheel about and turn about,
 And vex the world, they do,
The letters three, but most they love
 To plague the letters two.

There's some one checks his laughing spleen,
    And bends to us the three—
As oft he turns to us the two,
    And worships worthily.

Now fair befall the letters five,
    The letters three, and two :
In sooth it were a happy world
    If you had all your due.

ANSWER.

THE king, the statesman, churl, and knight,
The priest and thief agree :
They bow them low to letters three,
And worship Be-au-ty (B U T).

When rude rebellion o'er the land
Her wild confusion spreads,
With one consent all parties fly
For succour to Y Z's.

L'AMOUR FANFARON.

GARE, fainéant, sauve-toi, beaux yeux te regardent,
Péril t'environne—ah ! ses pieds lents trop se re-
tardent.

Mais enfin je le tiens—Merci, mignon, pour ce coup,
petite Claira,
Voici de nouvelles grâces, roses, lis, tant qu'il te
plaira.
Ha ! ha ! esprit moqueur, où s'enfuit donc ton allégresse ?
Point de ris, de calembourgs chez moi : réprime,
audacieux, ta hardiesse.
Jadis muet, t'adoucis, apprends-toi bien à soupirer.
Ha ! arrête-toi, dis-je, de ce lieu jamais on ne peut se
retirer.

Sache, étourdi, moi je suis grand Capitaine, veille toujours,

Cache des armes inévitables sous mes robes de
velours ;

Porte la guerre partout, partout sois toujours vain-
queur.

Ainsi je vais fixer la douleur à ton vilain cœur :

A genoux, scélérat, à moi ton hommage ; remplis le
destin.

De larmes, de peines, de peurs pour toi, ah, le beau
festin !

Crainte, Tristesse, Poésie, saisissez la perfide âme.

Holà !

Au secours ! vite, venez, tirez, frappez, arrachez
l'infâme—

Ah !

Peste, il s'en va !

E la fede degli amanti,

Come l' Araba Fenice,

Che vi sia, ciascun lo dice,

Dove sia, nessun lo sa !

Pietro Trapassi.

Like Arabia's Phœnix I

Reckon love's fidelity.

There's such a thing, we all confess ;

But where, not one of us can guess.

INFANS EXPOSITUS.

(Paraphrased from Crabbe's 'Foundling.')

QUISQUE dies curas, et habet lex plurima lites :
Neve togâ semper rura carent propriâ.
Infantem mater, sed plane in finibus, agris
Exposuit tacitis conscia sideribus.
Hic sibi nutrices, hic fisci publica cura
Jure suo mammas atque alimenta petit.
' Fama solo ingrediens caput inter nubila condit.'
Horrent vicani conveniuntque patres.
Multa monent multi, laudant, damnantque frequentes,
Discordique domus rumpitur eloquio.   10
Primum de facto ; verumne ? itane ?—ipse sibi infans
Testis adest : sole hoc clarius : at quid agant ?

Num vivit? digitis pinsus nimis undique duris,

    Ejulat improbulus : nec locus hic dubio est,

Dandum igitur nomen : multum res durior omnem

    Turbavit cœtum et per mora longa fuit.

Namque suum imprudens si quis concesserit, ' Euge ! '

    Audiat, 'ipse suum quam bene sustulerit ! '

Tum quantos æstus ! tum quanta silentia ! rursus

    Jurgia ! væ vivis unguibus ! at quid agant?   20

Vix acie hic aliquis tacite perstringere patres

    Ausus, ' cognomen quidni aliunde vacet ? '

Incipit effari, cum subvenit, ' Euge, caveto,

    Tutius absentes,' ergo iterum tenebræ,

Talia mussanti succurrit Pallas Athene

    E cœlo et passo crine manum implicuit,

Ut quondam impavido Peleïadæ Achileï,

    Et quiddam in patulas garriit auriculas.

Inde alacris dare consiliis sic lora secundas,

    Festinatque novas promere lætitias,   30

' O proceres faustis cura est adhibenda Calendis.

    Hæ nobis certo hoc certius expedient.

Hicce, malùm, nobis segetem monstravit iniquum ;

    Hicce dies nomen cedat et auspicium.'

'O lepidum ingenium,' confestim, 'o docta cerebri
  Congeries,' omnes 'o decus' ingeminant.
Jurgia sic tandem compostâ lite quiescunt,
  Sic timor ira cadunt, sic redit alma Themis.

.⁓.

THE PARISH REGISTER: BAPTISMS.

(From Crabbe's 'Village.')

To name an infant meet our village sires,
Assembled all as such event requires.
Frequent and full the rural sages sate,
And speakers many urged the long debate.
Some hardened knaves who roved the country round
Had left a babe within the parish bound
F.rst o tne ıact they questioned—Was it true ?
The child was brought. What then remained to
Was't dead or living ? This was fairly proved :
Twas pinched ; it roared, and every doubt removed. 10
Then by what name th' unwelcome guest to call
Was long a question, and it posed them all,
For he who lent it to a babe unknown,
Censorious men might take it for his own.

They looked about, they gravely spoke to all,
And not one Richard answered to the call.
Next they inquired the day when, passing by,
The unlucky peasant heard the stranger's cry.
This known, with all their words and work content,
Back to their homes the prudent vestry went   20
And Richard Monday to the workhouse sent.

AN ARABESQUE.

On living snow a dark and stately grove,
A silken thicket that the Graces wove
Long since, 'tis thought with song and potent charms
To hold ensnared a troubled world in arms ;
An arsenal, where Cupid keeps his bows,
Each ready bent, and set in glossy rows ;
An arch of triumph, or a bridge of sighs,
Where many a passing captive droops and dies ;
A fair-writ scroll, the crescent orb of night,
Darkening the gaze with its excessive light ;   10
A thundercloud, whence darting from beneath
Issue fierce lightnings carrying certain death.
By these true signs the sable banner know
Of the dread chief that holds his state below—
Man's deadliest foe, more dazzling than the morn,
Older than time, each passing hour new-born,

That in his crystal fortress, there reclined,

Sits at his ease and wars on all mankind.

Than him no fiercer savage walks the plain,

No stricken Herod, no ambitious Thane,   20

No bigot mother of an idiot king,

No lion's fang, no scorpion's fiery sting,

No honied words to gull a gaping league,

Such woes have proved a wicked world to plague.

E'en Mammon, the dull fiend that sins by rule,

Quotes Holy Writ, and makes his God his tool,

Bends when he comes ; slow gluttons gird them in,

Dance as he pipes, and learn a livelier mien.

His cruel form is tender as a girl's ;

And (save but hers) more rich his flowing curls.   30

Thief at all points, his glowing cheeks disclose

The stolen sweetness of the blushing rose ;

The upstart lilies that his temples bind

Look with disdain on those they left behind.

He whispers mischief, but that whisper seems

Like music faintly heard in happy dreams,

Where springing hopes and infant fancies wave

Their golden plumes ere life's lulled furies rave.

Winged like a sylph, all armed, with sparkling eyes

And winning smile, through heaven and earth he flies, 40

To quell a world ; half clad in flimsy gauze,

For spring perpetual in his train he draws ;

The little archer with dissembled care

Launches his shaft at random through the air ;

The tiny shrapnel in a thousand parts

Splits as it flies, and wounds a thousand hearts.

Yet simples heal : a mirror, or the shade

Of their sweet forms delightedly surveyed,

Sufficeth some ; or politics, or war,

Drink, or new wounds ; and some, the light cigar,   50

That calls the frolic spirits from their sleep,

That in the brain at watch and quarters keep,

Thence, as the mouth the trumpet sounds, at times

Pass in review and march in measured rhymes.

Pain flush in hearts : *der Freischütz*, each askew ;

Burnt faggots all—and he's his endings too—

' In one short day the longing heart grows old.'

' Sweet mother, I my shuttle cannot hold.'

'*Amico, ai vinto*'—and the boar

That slew Cythere's darling, baited sore   60

By puny boys, his tusks all burnt away,

Grunts full content through him the livelong day.

The bright-haired maid that bound her head with vows,

And lost no charm, was but his lure ; he ploughs

All fallows soon ; no fences keep him out.

Hosts of stern thoughts are ranked in vain ; no scout

But quits his post ; he sleeps not, but he seems

Colleagued with Mab, the lord of whirling dreams.

Read me my riddle.   He's a coming shade

On all who laugh ; by him are Edens made ;   70

From him the supple Frenchman learns his fence ;

The dance, the song are his ; shillelahs hence

Their touch and pressure ; calendars he makes

Of sullen fasts, and plaints of dismal aches,

Whereby his captives dwindle day by day

Sublime to gas and sigh themselves away,

Most like the filmy shapes, the slight impress

Idealised to gorgeous littleness,

Heroic art on patient canvas lays

Dares the broad day and winnies for her praise.   80

You of the glittering arms and lordly hall

And slumbering Beauty's bower, on you I call—

You that all subjects all at once can seize,

And write no verses though you rhyme with ease.[1]

Place me the bloody and luxurious Dane,

In mortal agony condemned again

To live his foul deeds through, to hear his crimes

Told slowly forth by Hamlet's tutored mimes ;

Place me the guilty eye, the cowering mien,

Like a lashed hound aside, the averted queen,   90

The rising doubt, the uneasy whisper round ;

The coward limbs that chain him to the ground ;

The desperate clutch, the wish but dread to fly ;

The ghostly shade, the avenger's living eye :

What draws the giddy sight? a pretty face,

An idle page, a scutcheon, or a lace.

Hold bias bowl—all services he apes,

Soothes lonely widows and takes off their crapes.

----

[1] Written in the lifetime of the distinguished artist her
referred to.

See how in rhyme, and sighing at his post,
The clerk engrossing is himself engrossed !   100
See the pale scholar in ambitious toil
O'er deep triangles spend the midnight oil ;
See how his tangents ruffle into curls,
His letters meet and whiten into pearls.
The circle to a beauteous oval grows,
Opes two blue eyes, and blushes like a rose ;
'Till all complete, the angel face appears
And loving ditties murmur in his ears.
Here tender maids long lives of sadness plan ;
All dressed in white, and all renouncing man.   110
Here withered elders make new wills and toy
Accepted lawyers there, burn *Coke* for joy.
In camp and court, in palace, cot, and hall,
The busy broker lots and sells us all.

NOTES TO THE ABOVE.

v. 57. Οἱ δὲ ποθεῦντες ἐν ἤματι γηράσκουσι.
                                        Theocritus.

v. 58. Γλύκεια μᾶτερ, οὔτοι δύναμαι κρέκειν τὸν ἴστον,
       Πόθῳ δάμεισα παῖδος βραδίναν δι' 'Αφρόδιταν.
                                        Sappho.

v. 59. Clorinda to Tancred.   *Tasso.*

v. 60. Ἄδωνιν ἡ Κυθήρη

ʼΩs εἶδε νεκρὸν ἤδη, κ.τ.λ.   *The Author—*

that is to say, not myself, but one of the Anacreons or Theocritus, as the case may be ; for the babe is something of a Richard
Monday (see above, p. 97), or foundling. I rather give my
censure against the latter myself, but unhistorically, and only
because it seems to me to resemble very much the style and
spirit of the former, and not at all that of the latter. When
these two do take the same subject,—as, for instance, Cupid
stung by a bee, the Ἔρως ποτ' ἐν ῥόδοισι, κ.τ.λ. of the former,
and the κηριοκλέπτης of the latter,—their similarity of treatment
is nothing very remarkable ; and, as in the serenade in ' Don
Giovanni,' Anacreon, the guitar, keeps saying one thing, and
Theocritus, the singer, another. This latter fellow for the most
part, whether scolding a king for shabbiness, praising a queen
for beauty, quarrelling among bumpkins, or cramming two
shrill shrews through a crowd, goes on pretty much in his
own pre-Virgilian way, and even in his heroics manages to
throw about them something of his accustomed farmhouse
simplicity.   In his ' Infant Hercules,' Alcmena washes her two
children, and fills them with milk—

Λούσασ' ἀμφοτέρους καὶ ἐμπλήσασα γάλακτος —

puts them to bed, sings them to sleep in first-rate nursery hexa-
meters, and so on ; hears great snakes in the nursery, violently
pinches up her husband, who rises, with something between a
parting snore and a groan, obediently, as he ought to do ; gropes
for his sword, which, like a gallant captain of yeomanry, he
always hangs at the head of his bed ; calls together the farm
servants, and the next morning sends for the priest, the blindest

he can find (Tiresias), to expound ; so that really, if the thing
was to have occurred, there is no earthly reason why it might
not have done so last week in one's own pet county, or why
Alcmena might not have worn a bodice and minever slippers
and sat to Leslie for his picture of the young mother ; for thus
it is, as Ulysses, of all men in the world (though, to be sure, the
real or Shakespeare Ulysses, and not the counterfeit of the
Athenian whig playwrights), says : ' One touch of nature makes
the whole world kin ; ' and so the past and present meet again,
and stone walls become a hermitage, and — and the mind
becomes amazingly vivid, for what have all these things to do
with Adonis ?

.<.

THE SICILIAN GOSSIPS.

(*From Theocritus.*)

SCENE.—*A crowd at a festival in ancient Alexandria.*

Μᾶ, πόθεν ὥνθρωπος; τί δὲ τὶν, εἰ κωτίλαι εἰμές ;
Πασάμενος ἐπίτασσε · Συρακοσίαις ἐπιτάσσεις ;
'Ως δ' εἰδῇς καὶ τοῦτο, Κορίνθιαι εἰμὲς ἄνωθεν,
'Ως καὶ ὁ Βελλεροφῶν. . . . κ.τ.λ.

HE.

Pray, hush for a few minutes, my good woman, the singing is very beautiful.

SHE.

Marry come up ! good woman indeed ! Who are you, I should like to know, to speak to us in that fashion ?

Go home and abuse your own lawful wife, if you have
one—and I am sure I pity her enough, poor
woman—do ; and don't talk to your betters and
fly into such a passion.

Who do you think is to care for you, you great
Cockney, going about cursing and swearing in
that sort of way, and you ought to be ashamed
of yourself, and me expecting who knows? like
a bull with a crumpled horn !

Police ! police ! Blame the fellows, they are never in
the way—and I'd have you to know we come
from Windsor, we do, where the Queen's Majesty
had her precious innocent babies born.

Aye, and we can span our own wrists too, and our
mothers afore us, which is more, I'll go bail, than
you can do, you great shambling, spindle-shanked
hoddy-doddy.

Ah ! you oaf, you jackanapes, you Herody reprobate !
you proud, percked-up squinting peacock !—Oh,
I'll burst ! why don't the brute answer a body ?

109

.⁓.

Apropos of Alcmena's nursery-song, the following, if only genuine, must be one of the earliest in existence, being apparently, from its reference to the Confusion of Tongues and the Income Tax, of the remotest possible Oriental antiquity.

Ἄρχετε ἐξ ὀβολούς, Μοῦσαι φίλαι, ἄρχετ᾽ ἀείδειν.

Ἄρχετε θυλάκιον βριξοφοροῦν τε λέγειν ·

Κίχλαι ἐν ἀρτοκρέᾳ ἔφριγεν δὶς δώδεκα πᾶσαι,

Τοῖσδ᾽ ἀναπεπταμένου γ᾽, εὐθὺ ἔμελπον ἅδην.

Οὔτι καλὸν τόδε θαῦμα, καλὴν τὴν δαιτὰ λέγωμεν

Ὀλβίῳ ἀνδρὶ πρέπειν, οὔτι πρέπειν βασιλεῖ ;

Χαίρετε, ὦ κιχλαι τε καὶ ἀρτόκρεας μέγα χαῖρε ·

Ὦ δεῖ πέντ᾽ ὀβολῶν οὐδὲν ἔτ᾽ ὕμμι μέλε.·

ς᾽

Spottiswoode & Co. Printers, New-street Square, London.

ـج

A LIST OF

KEGAN PAUL, TRENCH &

PUBLICATIONS.

1, *Paternoster Square,*
London.

A LIST OF

KEGAN PAUL, TRENCH & CO.'S PUBLICATIONS.

———————

CONTENTS.

GENERAL LITERATURE.

ADAMSON, H. T., B.D.—The Truth as it is in Jesus. Crown 8vo, 8s. 6d.

The Three Sevens. Crown 8vo, 5s. 6d.

The Millennium; or, The Mystery of God Finished. Crown 8vo, 6s.

A. K. H. B.—From a Quiet Place. A Volume of Sermons. Crown 8vo, 5s.

ALLEN, Rev. R., M.A.—Abraham: his Life, Times, and Travels, 3800 years ago. With Map. Second Edition. Post 8vo, 6s.

ALLIES, T. W., M.A.—Per Crucem ad Lucem. The Result of a Life. 2 vols. Demy 8vo, 25s.

A Life's Decision. Crown 8vo, 7s. 6d.

AMOS, Professor Sheldon.—The History and Principles of the Civil Law of Rome. An aid to the Study of Scientific and Comparative Jurisprudence. Demy 8vo. 16s.

ANDERDON, Rev. W. H.—Fasti Apostolici; a Chronology of the Years between the Ascension of our Lord and the Martyrdom of SS. Peter and Paul. Second Edition. Enlarged. Square 8vo, 5s.

Evenings with the Saints. Crown 8vo, 5s.

ANDERSON, David.—"Scenes" in the Commons. Crown 8vo, 5*s.*

ARMSTRONG, Richard A., B.A.—Latter-Day Teachers. Six Lectures. Small crown 8vo, 2*s.* 6*d.*

AUBERTIN, J. J.—A Flight to Mexico. With Seven full-page Illustrations and a Railway Map of Mexico. Crown 8vo, 7*s.* 6*d.*

BADGER, George Percy, D.C.L.—An English-Arabic Lexicon. In which the equivalent for English Words and Idiomatic Sentences are rendered into literary and colloquial Arabic. Royal 4to, 80*s.*

BAGEHOT, Walter.—The English Constitution. New and Revised Edition. Crown 8vo, 7*s.* 6*d.*

Lombard Street. A Description of the Money Market. Eighth Edition. Crown 8vo, 7*s.* 6*d.*

Essays on Parliamentary Reform. Crown 8vo, 5*s.*

Some Articles on the Depreciation of Silver, and Topics connected with it. Demy 8vo, 5*s.*

BAGENAL, Philip H.—The American-Irish and their Influence on Irish Politics. Crown 8vo, 5*s.*

BAGOT, Alan, C.E.—Accidents in Mines: their Causes and Prevention. Crown 8vo, 6*s.*

The Principles of Colliery Ventilation. Second Edition, greatly enlarged. Crown 8vo, 5*s.*

BAKER, Sir Sherston, Bart.—The Laws relating to Quarantine. Crown 8vo, 12*s.* 6*d.*

BALDWIN, Capt. J. H.—The Large and Small Game of Bengal and the North-Western Provinces of India. With 20 Illustrations. New and Cheaper Edition. Small 4to, 10*s.* 6*d.*

BALLIN, Ada S. and F. L.—A Hebrew Grammar. With Exercises selected from the Bible. Crown 8vo, 7*s.* 6*d.*

BARCLAY, Edgar.—Mountain Life in Algeria. With numerous Illustrations by Photogravure. Crown 4to, 16*s.*

BARLOW, James H.—The Ultimatum of Pessimism. An Ethical Study. Demy 8vo, 6*s.*

BARNES, William.—Outlines of Redecraft (Logic). With English Wording. Crown 8vo, 3*s.*

BAUR, Ferdinand, Dr. Ph.—A Philological Introduction to Greek and Latin for Students. Translated and adapted from the German, by C. KEGAN PAUL, M.A., and E. D. STONE, M.A. Third Edition. Crown 8vo, 6*s.*

BELLARS, Rev. W.—The Testimony of Conscience to the Truth and Divine Origin of the Christian Revelation. Burney Prize Essay. Small crown 8vo, 3*s.* 6*d.*

BELLINGHAM, Henry, M.P.—Social Aspects of Catholicism and Protestantism in their Civil Bearing upon Nations. Translated and adapted from the French of M. le BARON DE HAULLEVILLE. With a preface by His Eminence CARDINAL MANNING. Second and Cheaper Edition. Crown 8vo, 3*s.* 6*d.*

BELLINGHAM, H. Belsches Graham.—Ups and Downs of Spanish Travel. Second Edition. Crown 8vo, 5*s.*

BENN, Alfred W.—The Greek Philosophers. 2 vols. Demy 8vo, 28*s.*

BENT, J. Theodore.—Genoa : How the Republic Rose and Fell. With 18 Illustrations. Demy 8vo, 18*s.*

BLACKLEY, Rev. W. S.—Essays on Pauperism. 16mo. Cloth, 1*s.* 6*d.* ; sewed, 1*s.*

BLECKLEY, Henry. — Socrates and the Athenians : An Apology. Crown 8vo, 2*s.* 6*d.*

BLOOMFIELD, The Lady.—Reminiscences of Court and Diplomatic Life. With 3 Portraits and 6 Illustrations. Sixth Edition. 2 vols., 8vo, cloth, 28*s.*

*** New and Cheaper Edition. With Frontispiece. Crown 8vo, 6*s.*

BLUNT, The Ven. Archdeacon.—The Divine Patriot, and other Sermons. Preached in Scarborough and in Cannes. New and Cheaper Edition. Crown 8vo, 4*s.* 6*d.*

BLUNT, Wilfred S.—The Future of Islam. Crown 8vo, 6*s.*

BOOLE, Mary.—Symbolical Methods of Study. Crown 8vo, 5*s.*

BOUVERIE-PUSEY, S. E. B.—Permanence and Evolution. An Inquiry into the Supposed Mutability of Animal Types. Crown 8vo, 5*s.*

BOWEN, H. C., M.A.—Studies in English. For the use of Modern Schools. Seventh Thousand. Small crown 8vo, 1*s.* 6*d.*

English Grammar for Beginners. Fcap. 8vo, 1*s.*

BRADLEY, F. H.—The Principles of Logic. Demy 8vo, 16*s.*

BRIDGETT, Rev. T. E.—History of the Holy Eucharist in Great Britain. 2 vols. Demy 8vo, 18*s.*

BRODRICK, the Hon. G. C.—Political Studies. Demy 8vo, 14*s.*

BROOKE, Rev. S. A.—Life and Letters of the Late Rev. F. W. Robertson, M.A. Edited by.

    I. Uniform with Robertson's Sermons. 2 vols. With Steel Portrait. 7*s.* 6*d.*

    II. Library Edition. With Portrait. 8vo, 12*s.*

    III. A Popular Edition. In 1 vol., 8vo, 6*s.*

BROOKE, Rev. S. A.—Continued.

The Fight of Faith. Sermons preached on various occasions. Fifth Edition. Crown 8vo, 7s. 6d.

The Spirit of the Christian Life. New and Cheaper Edition. Crown 8vo, 5s.

Theology in the English Poets.—Cowper, Coleridge, Words-worth, and Burns. Fifth and Cheaper Edition. Post 8vo, 5s.

Christ in Modern Life. Sixteenth and Cheaper Edition. Crown 8vo, 5s.

Sermons. First Series. Thirteenth and Cheaper Edition. Crown 8vo, 5s.

Sermons. Second Series. Sixth and Cheaper Edition. Crown 8vo, 5s.

BROWN, Rev. J. Baldwin, B.A.—The Higher Life. Its Reality, Experience, and Destiny. Sixth Edition. Crown 8vo, 5s.

Doctrine of Annihilation in the Light of the Gospel of Love. Five Discourses. Fourth Edition. Crown 8vo, 2s. 6d.

The Christian Policy of Life. A Book for Young Men of Business. Third Edition. Crown 8vo, 3s. 6d.

BROWN, S. Borton, B.A.—The Fire Baptism of all Flesh; or, The Coming Spiritual Crisis of the Dispensation. Crown 8vo, 6s.

BROWN, Horatio F.—Life on the Lagoons. With two Illustrations and Map. Crown 8vo, 6s.

BROWNBILL, John.—Principles of English Canon Law. Part I. General Introduction. Crown 8vo, 6s.

BROWNE, W. R.—The Inspiration of the New Testament. With a Preface by the Rev. J. P. NORRIS, D.D. Fcap. 8vo, 2s. 6d.

BURDETT, Henry C.—Hints in Sickness—Where to Go and What to Do. Crown 8vo, 1s. 6d.

BURTON, Mrs. Richard.—The Inner Life of Syria, Palestine, and the Holy Land. Cheaper Edition in one volume. Large post 8vo. 7s. 6d.

BUSBECQ, Ogier Ghiselin de.—His Life and Letters. By CHARLES THORNTON FORSTER, M.A., and F. H. BLACKBURNE DANIELL, M.A. 2 vols. With Frontispieces. Demy 8vo, 24s.

CARPENTER, W. B., LL.D., M.D., F.R.S., etc.—The Principles of Mental Physiology. With their Applications to the Training and Discipline of the Mind, and the Study of its Morbid Conditions. Illustrated. Sixth Edition. 8vo, 12s.

Catholic Dictionary. Containing some account of the Doctrine, Discipline, Rites, Ceremonies, Councils, and Religious Orders of the Catholic Church. By WILLIAM E. ADDIS and THOMAS ARNOLD, M.A. Second Edition. Demy 8vo, 21s.

CERVANTES.—Journey to Parnassus. Spanish Text, with Translation into English Tercets, Preface, and Illustrative Notes, by JAMES Y. GIBSON. Crown 8vo, 12s.

CHEYNE, Rev. T. K.—The Prophecies of Isaiah. Translated with Critical Notes and Dissertations. 2 vols. Third Edition. Demy 8vo, 25s.

CLAIRAUT.—Elements of Geometry. Translated by Dr. KAINES. With 145 Figures. Crown 8vo, 4s. 6d.

CLAYDEN, P. W.—England under Lord Beaconsfield. The Political History of the Last Six Years, from the end of 1873 to the beginning of 1880. Second Edition, with Index and continuation to March, 1880. Demy 8vo, 16s.

Samuel Sharpe. Egyptologist and Translator of the Bible. Crown 8vo, 6s.

CLIFFORD, Samuel.—What Think Ye of the Christ? Crown 8vo, 6s.

CLODD, Edward, F.R.A.S.—The Childhood of the World : a Simple Account of Man in Early Times. Seventh Edition. Crown 8vo, 3s.
　　A Special Edition for Schools. 1s.

The Childhood of Religions. Including a Simple Account of the Birth and Growth of Myths and Legends. Eighth Thousand. Crown 8vo, 5s.
　　A Special Edition for Schools. 1s. 6d.

Jesus of Nazareth. With a brief sketch of Jewish History to the Time of His Birth. Small crown 8vo, 6s.

COGHLAN, J. Cole, D.D.—The Modern Pharisee and other Sermons. Edited by the Very Rev. H. H. DICKINSON, D.D., Dean of Chapel Royal, Dublin. New and Cheaper Edition. Crown 8vo, 7s. 6d.

COLERIDGE, Sara.—Memoir and Letters of Sara Coleridge. Edited by her Daughter. With Index. Cheap Edition. With Portrait. 7s. 6d.

Collects Exemplified. Being Illustrations from the Old and New Testaments of the Collects for the Sundays after Trinity. By the Author of "A Commentary on the Epistles and Gospels." Edited by the Rev. JOSEPH JACKSON. Crown 8vo, 5s.

CONNELL, A. K.—Discontent and Danger in India. Small crown 8vo, 3s. 6d.

The Economic Revolution of India. Crown 8vo, 4s. 6d.

CORY, William.—A Guide to Modern English History. Part I. —MDCCCXV.-MDCCCXXX. Demy 8vo, 9s. Part II.— MDCCCXXX.-MDCCCXXXV., 15s.

COTTERILL, H. B.—An Introduction to the Study of Poetry. Crown 8vo, 7s. 6d.

COX, Rev. Sir George W., M.A., Bart.—A History of Greece from the Earliest Period to the end of the Persian War. New Edition. 2 vols. Demy 8vo, 36s.

The Mythology of the Aryan Nations. New Edition. Demy 8vo, 16s.

Tales of Ancient Greece. New Edition. Small crown 8vo, 6s.

A Manual of Mythology in the form of Question and Answer. New Edition. Fcap. 8vo, 3s.

An Introduction to the Science of Comparative Mythology and Folk-Lore. Second Edition. Crown 8vo. 7s. 6d.

COX, Rev. Sir G. W., M.A., Bart., and JONES, Eustace Hinton.— Popular Romances of the Middle Ages. Third Edition, in 1 vol. Crown 8vo, 6s.

COX, Rev. Samuel, D.D.—Salvator Mundi ; or, Is Christ the Saviour of all Men ? Eighth Edition. Crown 8vo, 5s.

The Genesis of Evil, and other Sermons, mainly expository. Third Edition. Crown 8vo, 6s.

A Commentary on the Book of Job. With a Translation. Demy 8vo, 15s.

The Larger Hope. A Sequel to "Salvator Mundi." 16mo, 1s.

CRAVEN, Mrs.—A Year's Meditations. Crown 8vo, 6s.

CRAWFURD, Oswald.—Portugal, Old and New. With Illustrations and Maps. New and Cheaper Edition. Crown 8vo, 6s.

CROZIER, John Beattie, M.B.—The Religion of the Future. Crown 8vo, 6s.

DANIELL, Clarmont.—The Gold Treasure of India. An Inquiry into its Amount, the Cause of its Accumulation, and the Proper Means of using it as Money. Crown 8vo, 5s.

Darkness and Dawn : the Peaceful Birth of a New Age. Small crown 8vo, 2s 6d.

DAVIDSON, Rev. Samuel, D.D., LL.D.—Canon of the Bible : Its Formation, History, and Fluctuations. Third and Revised Edition. Small crown 8vo, 5s.

The Doctrine of Last Things contained in the New Testament compared with the Notions of the Jews and the Statements of Church Creeds. Small crown 8vo, 3s. 6d.

DAVIDSON, Thomas.—The Parthenon Frieze, and other Essays. Crown 8vo, 6s.

DAWSON, Geo., M.A. Prayers, with a Discourse on Prayer. Edited by his Wife. First Series. Eighth Edition. Crown 8vo, 6s.

Prayers, with a Discourse on Prayer. Edited by GEORGE ST. CLAIR. Second Series. Crown 8vo, 6s.

DAWSON, Geo., M.A.—continued.

Sermons on Disputed Points and Special Occasions. Edited by his Wife. Fourth Edition. Crown 8vo, 6s.

Sermons on Daily Life and Duty. Edited by his Wife. Fourth Edition. Crown 8vo, 6s.

The Authentic Gospel, and other Sermons. Edited by GEORGE ST. CLAIR. Third Edition. Crown 8vo, 6s.

Three Books of God : Nature, History, and Scripture. Sermons edited by GEORGE ST. CLAIR. Crown 8vo, 6s.

DE JONCOURT, Madame Marie.—**Wholesome Cookery.** Second Edition. Crown 8vo, 3s. 6d.

DE LONG, Lieut. Com. G. W.—**The Voyage of the Jeannette.** The Ship and Ice Journals of. Edited by his Wife, EMMA DE LONG. With Portraits, Maps, and many Illustrations on wood and stone. 2 vols. Demy 8vo, 36s.

DESPREZ, Philip S., B.D.—**Daniel and John** ; or, The Apocalypse of the Old and that of the New Testament. Demy 8vo, 12s.

DEVEREUX, W. Cope, R.N., F.R.G.S.—**Fair Italy, the Riviera, and Monte Carlo.** Comprising a Tour through North and South Italy and Sicily, with a short account of Malta. Crown 8vo, 6s.

DOWDEN, Edward, LL.D.—**Shakspere :** a Critical Study of his Mind and Art. Seventh Edition. Post 8vo, 12s.

Studies in Literature, 1789–1877. Third Edition. Large post 8vo, 6s.

DUFFIELD, A. J.—**Don Quixote : his Critics and Commentators.** With a brief account of the minor works of MIGUEL DE CERVANTES SAAVEDRA, and a statement of the aim and end of the greatest of them all. A handy book for general readers. Crown 8vo, 3s. 6d.

DU MONCEL, Count.—**The Telephone, the Microphone, and the Phonograph.** With 74 Illustrations. Second Edition. Small crown 8vo, 5s.

DURUY, Victor.—**History of Rome and the Roman People.** Edited by Prof. MAHAFFY. With nearly 3000 Illustrations. 4to. Vol. I. in 2 parts, 30s.

EDGEWORTH, F. Y.—**Mathematical Psychics.** An Essay on the Application of Mathematics to Social Science. Demy 8vo, 7s. 6d.

Educational Code of the Prussian Nation, in its Present Form. In accordance with the Decisions of the Common Provincial Law, and with those of Recent Legislation. Crown 8vo, 2s. 6d.

Education Library. Edited by PHILIP MAGNUS :—

An Introduction to the History of Educational Theories. By OSCAR BROWNING, M.A. Second Edition. 3s. 6d.

Old Greek Education. By the Rev. Prof. MAHAFFY, M.A. Second Edition. 3s. 6d.

School Management. Including a general view of the work of Education, Organization and Discipline. By JOSEPH LANDON. Third Edition. 6s.

Eighteenth Century Essays. Selected and Edited by AUSTIN DOBSON. With a Miniature Frontispiece by R. Caldecott. Parchment Library Edition, 6s. ; vellum, 7s. 6d.

ELSDALE, Henry.—Studies in Tennyson's Idylls. Crown 8vo, 5s.

ELYOT, Sir Thomas.—The Boke named the Gouernour. Edited from the First Edition of 1531 by HENRY HERBERT STEPHEN CROFT, M.A., Barrister-at-Law. With Portraits of Sir Thomas and Lady Elyot, copied by permission of her Majesty from Holbein's Original Drawings at Windsor Castle. 2 vols. Fcap. 4to, 50s.

Enoch the Prophet. The Book of. Archbishop LAURENCE'S Translation, with an Introduction by the Author of " The Evolution of Christianity." Crown 8vo, 5s.

Eranus. A Collection of Exercises in the Alcaic and Sapphic Metres. Edited by F. W. CORNISH, Assistant Master at Eton. Second Edition. Crown 8vo, 2s.

EVANS, Mark.—The Story of Our Father's Love, told to Children. Sixth and Cheaper Edition. With Four Illustrations. Fcap. 8vo, 1s. 6d.

A Book of Common Prayer and Worship for Household Use, compiled exclusively from the Holy Scriptures. Second Edition. Fcap. 8vo, 1s.

The Gospel of Home Life. Crown 8vo, 4s. 6d.

The King's Story-Book. In Three Parts. Fcap. 8vo, 1s. 6d. each.

** Parts I. and II. with Eight Illustrations and Two Picture Maps, now ready.

" Fan Kwae " at Canton before Treaty Days 1825-1844. By an old Resident. With Frontispiece. Crown 8vo, 5s.

FLECKER, Rev. Eliezer.—Scripture Onomatology. Being Critical Notes on the Septuagint and other Versions. Second Edition. Crown 8vo, 3s. 6d.

FLOREDICE, W. H.—A Month among the Mere Irish. Small crown 8vo, 5s.

FOWLE, Rev. T. W.—The Divine Legation of Christ. Crown 8vo, 7s.

FULLER, Rev. Morris.—The Lord's Day ; or, Christian Sunday. Its Unity, History, Philosophy, and Perpetual Obligation. Sermons. Demy 8vo, 10s. 6d.

GARDINER, Samuel R., and J. BASS MULLINGER, M.A.— Introduction to the Study of English History. Second Edition. Large crown 8vo, 9s.

GARDNER, Dorsey.—Quatre Bras, Ligny, and Waterloo. A Narrative of the Campaign in Belgium, 1815. With Maps and Plans. Demy 8vo, 16s.

Genesis in Advance of Present Science. A Critical Investigation of Chapters I.-IX. By a Septuagenarian Beneficed Presbyter. Demy 8vo. 10s. 6d.

GENNA, E. — Irresponsible Philanthropists. Being some Chapters on the Employment of Gentlewomen. Small crown 8vo, 2s. 6d.

GEORGE, Henry.—Progress and Poverty : An Inquiry into the Causes of Industrial Depressions, and of Increase of Want with Increase of Wealth. The Remedy. Fifth Library Edition. Post 8vo, 7s. 6d. Cabinet Edition. Crown 8vo, 2s. 6d. Also a Cheap Edition. Limp cloth, 1s. 6d. Paper covers, 1s.

Social Problems. Fourth Thousand. Crown 8vo, 5s. Cheap Edition. Sewed, 1s.

GIBSON, James Y. – Journey to Parnassus. Composed by MIGUEL DE CERVANTES SAAVEDRA. Spanish Text, with Translation into English Tercets, Preface, and Illustrative Notes, by. Crown 8vo, 12s.

Glossary of Terms and Phrases. Edited by the Rev. H. PERCY SMITH and others. Medium 8vo, 12s.

GLOVER, F., M.A.—Exempla Latina. A First Construing Book, with Short Notes, Lexicon, and an Introduction to the Analysis of Sentences. Second Edition. Fcap. 8vo, 2s.

GOLDSMID, Sir Francis Henry, Bart., Q.C., M.P.—Memoir of. With Portrait. Second Edition, Revised. Crown 8vo, 6s.

GOODENOUGH, Commodore J. G.—Memoir of, with Extracts from his Letters and Journals. Edited by his Widow. With Steel Engraved Portrait. Third Edition. Crown 8vo, 5s.

GOSSE, Edmund W.—Studies in the Literature of Northern Europe. With a Frontispiece designed and etched by Alma Tadema. New and Cheaper Edition. Large crown 8vo, 6s.

Seventeenth Century Studies. A Contribution to the History of English Poetry. Demy 8vo, 10s. 6d.

GOULD, Rev. S. Baring, M.A.—Germany, Present and Past. New and Cheaper Edition. Large crown 8vo, 7s. 6d.

GOWAN, Major Walter E.—A. Ivanoff's Russian Grammar. (16th Edition.) Translated, enlarged, and arranged for use of Students of the Russian Language. Demy 8vo, 6s.

GOWER, Lord Ronald. My Reminiscences. Second Edition. 2 vols. With Frontispieces. Demy 8vo, 30s.

⁎⁎⁎ Also a Cheap Edition. With Portraits. Large crown 8vo, 7s. 6d.

GRAHAM, William, M.A.—The Creed of Science, Religious, Moral, and Social. Second Edition, Revised. Crown 8vo, 6s.

GRIFFITH, Thomas, A.M.—The Gospel of the Divine Life : a Study of the Fourth Evangelist. Demy 8vo, 14s.

GRIMLEY, Rev. H. N., M.A.—Tremadoc Sermons, chiefly on the Spiritual Body, the Unseen World, and the Divine Humanity. Fourth Edition. Crown 8vo, 6s.

G. S. B.—A Study of the Prologue and Epilogue in English Literature from Shakespeare to Dryden. Crown 8vo, 5s.

GUSTAFSON, A.—The Foundation of Death. Crown 8vo.

HAECKEL, Prof. Ernst.—The History of Creation. Translation revised by Professor E. RAY LANKESTER, M.A., F.R.S. With Coloured Plates and Genealogical Trees of the various groups of both Plants and Animals. 2 vols. Third Edition. Post 8vo, 32s.

The History of the Evolution of Man. With numerous Illustrations. 2 vols. Post 8vo, 32s.

A Visit to Ceylon. Post 8vo, 7s. 6d.

Freedom in Science and Teaching. With a Prefatory Note by T. H. HUXLEY, F.R.S. Crown 8vo, 5s.

HALF-CROWN SERIES :—

A Lost Love. By ANNA C. OGLE [Ashford Owen].

Sister Dora : a Biography. By MARGARET LONSDALE.

True Words for Brave Men : a Book for Soldiers and Sailors. By the late CHARLES KINGSLEY.

Notes of Travel : being Extracts from the Journals of Count VON MOLTKE.

English Sonnets. Collected and Arranged by J. DENNIS.

London Lyrics. By F. LOCKER.

Home Songs for Quiet Hours. By the Rev. Canon R. H. BAYNES.

HARROP, Robert.—Bolingbroke. A Political Study and Criticism. Demy 8vo, 14s.

HART, Rev. J. W. T.—The Autobiography of Judas Iscariot. A Character Study. Crown 8vo, 3s. 6d.

HAWEIS, Rev. H. R., M.A.—Current Coin. Materialism—The Devil—Crime—Drunkenness—Pauperism—Emotion—Recreation—The Sabbath. Fifth and Cheaper Edition. Crown 8vo, 5*s*.

Arrows in the Air. Fifth and Cheaper Edition. Crown 8vo, 5*s*.

Speech in Season. Fifth and Cheaper Edition. Crown 8vo, 5*s*.

Thoughts for the Times. Thirteenth and Cheaper Edition. Crown 8vo, 5*s*.

Unsectarian Family Prayers. New and Cheaper Edition. Fcap. 8vo, 1*s*. 6*d*.

HAWKINS, Edwards Comerford.—Spirit and Form. Sermons preached in the Parish Church of Leatherhead. Crown 8vo, 6*s*.

HAWTHORNE, Nathaniel.—Works. Complete in Twelve Volumes. Large post 8vo, 7*s*. 6*d*. each volume.

VOL. I. TWICE-TOLD TALES.
II. MOSSES FROM AN OLD MANSE.
III. THE HOUSE OF THE SEVEN GABLES, AND THE SNOW IMAGE.
IV. THE WONDERBOOK, TANGLEWOOD TALES, AND GRAND-FATHER'S CHAIR.
V. THE SCARLET LETTER, AND THE BLITHEDALE ROMANCE.
VI. THE MARBLE FAUN. [Transformation.]
VII. ⎫
VIII. ⎬ OUR OLD HOME, AND ENGLISH NOTE-BOOKS.
IX. AMERICAN NOTE-BOOKS.
X. FRENCH AND ITALIAN NOTE-BOOKS.
XI. SEPTIMIUS FELTON, THE DOLLIVER ROMANCE, FANSHAWE, AND, IN AN APPENDIX, THE ANCESTRAL FOOTSTEP.
XII. TALES AND ESSAYS, AND OTHER PAPERS, WITH A BIO-GRAPHICAL SKETCH OF HAWTHORNE.

HAYES, A. A., Junr.—New Colorado, and the Santa Fé Trail. With Map and 60 Illustrations. Square 8vo, 9*s*.

HENNESSY, Sir John Pope.—Ralegh in Ireland. With his Letters on Irish Affairs and some Contemporary Documents. Large crown 8vo, printed on hand-made paper, parchment, 10*s*. 6*d*.

HENRY, Philip.—Diaries and Letters of. Edited by MATTHEW HENRY LEE, M.A. Large crown 8vo, 7*s*. 6*d*.

HIDE, Albert.—The Age to Come. Small crown 8vo, 2*s*. 6*d*.

HIME, Major H. W. L., R.A.—Wagnerism : A Protest. Crown 8vo, 2*s*. 6*d*.

HINTON, J.—Life and Letters. Edited by ELLICE HOPKINS, with an Introduction by Sir W. W. GULL, Bart., and Portrait engraved on Steel by C. H. Jeens. Fourth Edition. Crown 8vo, 8*s*. 6*d*.

Philosophy and Religion. Second Edition. Crown 8vo, 5*s*.

The Law Breaker. Crown 8vo.

HINTON, J.—continued.

The Mystery of Pain. New Edition. Fcap. 8vo, 1s.

Hodson of Hodson's Horse ; or, Twelve Years of a Soldier's Life in India. Being extracts from the Letters of the late Major W. S. R. Hodson. With a Vindication from the Attack of Mr. Bosworth Smith. Edited by his brother, G. H. HODSON, M.A. Fourth Edition. Large crown 8vo, 5s.

*HOLTHAM, E. G.—*Eight Years in Japan, 1873–1881. Work, Travel, and Recreation. With three Maps. Large crown 8vo, 9s.

*HOOPER, Mary.—*Little Dinners: How to Serve them with Elegance and Economy. Eighteenth Edition. Crown 8vo, 2s. 6d.

Cookery for Invalids, Persons of Delicate Digestion, and Children. Third Edition. Crown 8vo, 2s. 6d.

Every-Day Meals. Being Economical and Wholesome Recipes for Breakfast, Luncheon, and Supper. Fifth Edition. Crown 8vo, 2s. 6d.

*HOPKINS, Ellice.—*Life and Letters of James Hinton, with an Introduction by Sir W. W. GULL, Bart., and Portrait engraved on Steel by C. H. Jeens. Fourth Edition. Crown 8vo, 8s. 6d.

Work amongst Working Men. Fifth Edition. Crown 8vo, 3s. 6d.

*HOSPITALIER, E.—*The Modern Applications of Electricity. Translated and Enlarged by JULIUS MAIER, Ph.D. 2 vols. Second Edition, Revised, with many additions and numerous Illustrations. Demy 8vo, 12s. 6d. each volume.
VOL. I.—Electric Generators, Electric Light.
VOL. II.—Telephone : Various Applications : Electrical Transmission of Energy.

Household Readings on Prophecy. By a Layman. Small crown 8vo, 3s. 6d.

*HUGHES, Henry.—*The Redemption of the World. Crown 8vo, 3s. 6d.

*HUNTINGFORD, Rev. E., D.C.L.—*The Apocalypse. With a Commentary and Introductory Essay. Demy 8vo, 5s.

*HUTTON, Arthur, M.A.—*The Anglican Ministry : Its Nature and Value in relation to the Catholic Priesthood. With a Preface by His Eminence CARDINAL NEWMAN. Demy 8vo, 14s.

*HUTTON, Rev. C. F.—*Unconscious Testimony ; or, The Silent Witness of the Hebrew to the Truth of the Historical Scriptures. Crown 8vo, 2s. 6d.

*HYNDMAN, H. M.—*The Historical Basis of Socialism in England. Large crown 8vo, 8s. 6d.

IM THURN, Everard F.—Among the Indians of Guiana. Being Sketches, chiefly anthropologic, from the Interior of British Guiana. With 53 Illustrations and a Map. Demy 8vo, 18s.

Jaunt in a Junk : A Ten Days' Cruise in Indian Seas. Large crown 8vo, 7s. 6d.

JENKINS, E., and RAYMOND, J.—The Architect's Legal Handbook. Third Edition, Revised. Crown 8vo, 6s.

JENNINGS, Mrs. Vaughan.—Rahel : Her Life and Letters. Large post 8vo, 7s. 6d.

JERVIS, Rev. W. Henley.—The Gallican Church and the Revolution. A Sequel to the History of the Church of France, from the Concordat of Bologna to the Revolution. Demy 8vo, 18s.

JOEL, L.—A Consul's Manual and Shipowner's and Ship-master's Practical Guide in their Transactions Abroad. With Definitions of Nautical, Mercantile, and Legal Terms ; a Glossary of Mercantile Terms in English, French, German, Italian, and Spanish ; Tables of the Money, Weights, and Measures of the Principal Commercial Nations and their Equivalents in British Standards ; and Forms of Consular and Notarial Acts. Demy 8vo, 12s.

JOHNSTONE, C. F., M.A.—Historical Abstracts : being Outlines of the History of some of the less known States of Europe. Crown 8vo, 7s. 6d.

JOLLY, William, F.R.S.E., etc.—The Life of John Duncan, Scotch Weaver and Botanist. With Sketches of his Friends and Notices of his Times. Second Edition. Large crown 8vo, with etched portrait, 9s.

JONES, C. A.—The Foreign Freaks of Five Friends. With 30 Illustrations. Crown 8vo, 6s.

JOYCE, P. W., LL.D., etc.—Old Celtic Romances. Translated from the Gaelic. Crown 8vo, 7s. 6d.

JOYNES, J. L.—The Adventures of a Tourist in Ireland. Second edition. Small crown 8vo, 2s. 6d.

KAUFMANN, Rev. M., B.A.—Socialism : its Nature, its Dangers, and its Remedies considered. Crown 8vo, 7s. 6d.

    Utopias ; or, Schemes of Social Improvement, from Sir Thomas More to Karl Marx. Crown 8vo, 5s.

KAY, David, F.R.G.S.—Education and Educators. Crown 8vo, 7s. 6d.

KAY, Joseph.—Free Trade in Land. Edited by his Widow. With Preface by the Right Hon. JOHN BRIGHT, M.P. Seventh Edition. Crown 8vo, 5s.

KEMPIS, Thomas à.—**Of the Imitation of Christ.** Parchment Library Edition.—Parchment or cloth, 6s. ; vellum, 7s. 6d. The Red Line Edition, fcap. 8vo, red edges, 2s. 6d. The Cabinet Edition, small 8vo, cloth limp, 1s. ; cloth boards, red edges, 1s. 6d. The Miniature Edition, red edges, 32mo, 1s.

⁎⁎⁎ All the above Editions may be had in various extra bindings.

KENT, C.—**Corona Catholica ad Petri successoris Pedes Oblata. De Summi Pontificis Leonis XIII. Assumptione Epigramma.** In Quinquaginta Linguis. Fcap. 4to, 15s.

KETTLEWELL, Rev. S.—**Thomas à Kempis and the Brothers of Common Life.** 2 vols. With Frontispieces. Demy 8vo, 30s.

KIDD, Joseph, M.D.—**The Laws of Therapeutics ;** or, the Science and Art of Medicine. Second Edition. Crown 8vo, 6s.

KINGSFORD, Anna, M.D.—**The Perfect Way in Diet.** A Treatise advocating a Return to the Natural and Ancient Food of our Race. Small crown 8vo, 2s.

KINGSLEY, Charles, M.A.—**Letters and Memories of his Life.** Edited by his Wife. With two Steel Engraved Portraits, and Vignettes on Wood. Fourteenth Cabinet Edition. 2 vols. Crown 8vo, 12s.

⁎⁎⁎ Also a People's Edition, in one volume. With Portrait. Crown 8vo, 6s.

All Saints' Day, and other Sermons. Edited by the Rev. W. HARRISON. Third Edition. Crown 8vo, 7s. 6d.

True Words for Brave Men. A Book for Soldiers' and Sailors' Libraries. Tenth Edition. Crown 8vo, 2s. 6d.

KNOX, Alexander A.—**The New Playground ;** or, Wanderings in Algeria. New and cheaper edition. Large crown 8vo, 6s.

LANDON, Joseph.—**School Management ;** Including a General View of the Work of Education, Organization, and Discipline. Third Edition. Crown 8vo, 6s.

LAURIE, S. S.—**The Training of Teachers,** and other Educational Papers. Crown 8vo, 7s. 6d.

LEE, Rev. F. G., D.C.L.—**The Other World ;** or, Glimpses of the Supernatural. 2 vols. A New Edition. Crown 8vo, 15s.

Letters from a Young Emigrant in Manitoba. Second Edition. Small crown 8vo, 3s. 6d.

LEWIS, Edward Dillon.—**A Draft Code of Criminal Law and Procedure.** Demy 8vo, 21s.

LILLIE, Arthur, M.R.A.S.—**The Popular Life of Buddha.** Containing an Answer to the Hibbert Lectures of 1881. With Illustrations. Crown 8vo, 6s.

LLOYD, Walter.—The Hope of the World : An Essay on Universal Redemption. Crown 8vo, 5s.

LONSDALE, Margaret.—Sister Dora : a Biography. With Portrait. Twenty-seventh Edition. Crown 8vo, 2s. 6d.

LOUNSBURY, Thomas R.—James Fenimore Cooper. Crown 8vo, 5s.

LOWDER, Charles.—A Biography. By the Author of " St. Teresa." New and Cheaper Edition. Crown 8vo. With Portrait. 3s. 6d.

LYTTON, Edward Bulwer, Lord.—Life, Letters and Literary Remains. By his Son, the EARL OF LYTTON. With Portraits, Illustrations and Facsimiles. Demy 8vo. Vols. I. and II., 32s.

MACAULAY, G. C.—Francis Beaumont : A Critical Study. Crown 8vo, 5s.

MAC CALLUM, M. W.—Studies in Low German and High German Literature. Crown 8vo, 6s.

MACDONALD, George. — Donal Grant. A New Novel. 3 vols. Crown 8vo, 31s. 6d.

MACHIAVELLI, Niccolò. — Life and Times. By Prof. Villari. Translated by Linda Villari. 4 vols. Large post, 8vo, 48s.

MACHIAVELLI, Niccolò.—Discourses on the First Decade of Titus Livius. Translated from the Italian by NINIAN HILL THOMSON, M.A. Large crown 8vo, 12s.

The Prince. Translated from the Italian by N. H. T. Small crown 8vo, printed on hand-made paper, bevelled boards, 6s.

MACKENZIE, Alexander.—How India is Governed. Being an Account of England's Work in India. Small crown 8vo, 2s.

MACNAUGHT, Rev. John.—Cœna Domini : An Essay on the Lord's Supper, its Primitive Institution, Apostolic Uses, and Subsequent History. Demy 8vo, 14s.

MACWALTER, Rev. G. S.—Life of Antonio Rosmini Serbati (Founder of the Institute of Charity). 2 vols. Demy 8vo. [Vol. I. now ready, price 12s.

MAGNUS, Mrs.—About the Jews since Bible Times. From the Babylonian Exile till the English Exodus. Small crown 8vo, 6s.

MAIR, R. S., M.D., F.R.C.S.E.—The Medical Guide for Anglo-Indians. Being a Compendium of Advice to Europeans in India, relating to the Preservation and Regulation of Health. With a Supplement on the Management of Children in India. Second Edition. Crown 8vo, limp cloth, 3s. 6d.

MALDEN, Henry Elliot.—Vienna, 1683. The History and Consequences of the Defeat of the Turks before Vienna, September 12th, 1683, by John Sobieski, King of Poland, and Charles Leopold, Duke of Lorraine. Crown 8vo, 4s. 6d.

Many Voices. A volume of Extracts from the Religious Writers of Christendom from the First to the Sixteenth Century. With Biographical Sketches. Crown 8vo, cloth extra, red edges, 6s.

MARKHAM, Capt. Albert Hastings, R.N.—The Great Frozen Sea : A Personal Narrative of the Voyage of the *Alert* during the Arctic Expedition of 1875-6. With 6 Full-page Illustrations, 2 Maps, and 27 Woodcuts. Sixth and Cheaper Edition. Crown 8vo, 6s.

A Polar Reconnaissance : being the Voyage of the *Isbjörn* to Novaya Zemlya in 1879. With 10 Illustrations. Demy 8vo, 16s.

Marriage and Maternity ; or, Scripture Wives and Mothers. Small crown 8vo, 4s. 6d.

MARTINEAU, Gertrude.—Outline Lessons on Morals. Small crown 8vo, 3s. 6d.

MAUDSLEY, H., M.D.—Body and Will. Being an Essay concerning Will, in its Metaphysical, Physiological, and Pathological Aspects. 8vo, 12s.

McGRATH, Terence.—Pictures from Ireland. New and Cheaper Edition. Crown 8vo, 2s.

MEREDITH, M.A.—Theotokos, the Example for Woman. Dedicated, by permission, to Lady Agnes Wood. Revised by the Venerable Archdeacon DENISON. 32mo, limp cloth, 1s. 6d.

MILLER, Edward.—The History and Doctrines of Irvingism ; or, The so-called Catholic and Apostolic Church. 2 vols. Large post 8vo, 25s.

The Church in Relation to the State. Large crown 8vo, 7s. 6d.

MINCHIN, J. G.—Bulgaria since the War : Notes of a Tour in the Autumn of 1879. Small crown 8vo, 3s. 6d.

MITCHELL, Lucy M.—A History of Ancient Sculpture. With numerous Illustrations, including 6 Plates in Phototype. Super royal 8vo, 42s.

Selections from Ancient Sculpture. Being a Portfolio containing Reproductions in Phototype of 36 Masterpieces of Ancient Art to illustrate Mrs. Mitchell's " History of Ancient Sculpture." 18s.

MITFORD, Bertram.—Through the Zulu Country. Its Battlefields and its People. With five Illustrations. Demy 8vo, 14s.

MOCKLER, E.—A Grammar of the Baloochee Language, as it is spoken in Makran (Ancient Gedrosia), in the Persia-Arabic and Roman characters. Fcap. 8vo, 5s.

MOLESWORTH, Rev. W. Nassau, M.A.—History of the Church of England from 1660. Large crown 8vo, 7s. 6d.

MORELL, J. R.—Euclid Simplified in Method and Language. Being a Manual of Geometry. Compiled from the most important French Works, approved by the University of Paris and the Minister of Public Instruction. Fcap. 8vo, 2s. 6d.

MORRIS, George.—The Duality of all Divine Truth in our Lord Jesus Christ. For God's Self-manifestation in the Impartation of the Divine Nature to Man. Large crown 8vo, 7s. 6d.

MORSE, E. S., Ph.D.—First Book of Zoology. With numerous Illustrations. New and Cheaper Edition. Crown 8vo, 2s. 6d.

MURPHY, John Nicholas.—The Chair of Peter; or, The Papacy considered in its Institution, Development, and Organization, and in the Benefits which for over Eighteen Centuries it has conferred on Mankind. Demy 8vo, 18s.

My Ducats and My Daughter. A New Novel. 3 vols. Crown 8vo, 31s. 6d.

NELSON, J. H., M.A.—A Prospectus of the Scientific Study of the Hindû Law. Demy 8vo, 9s.

NEWMAN, Cardinal.—Characteristics from the Writings of. Being Selections from his various Works. Arranged with the Author's personal Approval. Sixth Edition. With Portrait. Crown 8vo, 6s.

*** A Portrait of Cardinal Newman, mounted for framing, can be had, 2s. 6d.

NEWMAN, Francis William.—Essays on Diet. Small crown 8vo, cloth limp, 2s.

New Truth and the Old Faith: Are they Incompatible? By a Scientific Layman. Demy 8vo, 10s. 6d.

New Werther. By LOKI. Small crown 8vo, 2s. 6d.

NICHOLSON, Edward Byron.—The Gospel according to the Hebrews. Its Fragments Translated and Annotated, with a Critical Analysis of the External and Internal Evidence relating to it. Demy 8vo, 9s. 6d.

A New Commentary on the Gospel according to Matthew. Demy 8vo, 12s.

NICOLS, Arthur, F.G.S., F.R.G.S.—Chapters from the Physical History of the Earth: an Introduction to Geology and Palæontology. With numerous Illustrations. Crown 8vo, 5s.

NOPS, Marianne.—Class Lessons on Euclid. Part I. containing the First Two Books of the Elements. Crown 8vo, 2s. 6d.

Notes on St. Paul's Epistle to the Galatians. For Readers of the Authorized Version or the Original Greek. Demy 8vo, 2s. 6d.

Nuces : EXERCISES ON THE SYNTAX OF THE PUBLIC SCHOOL LATIN PRIMER. New Edition in Three Parts. Crown 8vo, each 1s.
*** The Three Parts can also be had bound together, 3s.

OATES, Frank, F.R.G.S.—Matabele Land and the Victoria Falls. A Naturalist's Wanderings in the Interior of South Africa. Edited by C. G. OATES, B.A. With numerous Illustrations and 4 Maps. Demy 8vo, 21s.

OGLE, W., M.D., F.R.C.P.—Aristotle on the Parts of Animals. Translated, with Introduction and Notes. Royal 8vo, 12s. 6d.

O'HAGAN, Lord, K.P. — Occasional Papers and Addresses. Large crown 8vo, 7s. 6d.

OKEN, Lorenz, Life of. By ALEXANDER ECKER. With Explanatory Notes, Selections from Oken's Correspondence, and Portrait of the Professor. From the German by ALFRED TULK. Crown 8vo, 6s.

O'MEARA, Kathleen.—Frederic Ozanam, Professor of the Sorbonne : His Life and Work. Second Edition. Crown 8vo, 7s. 6d.

Henri Perreyve and his Counsels to the Sick. Small crown 8vo, 5s.

OSBORNE, Rev. W. A.—The Revised Version of the New Testament. A Critical Commentary, with Notes upon the Text. Crown 8vo, 5s.

OTTLEY, H. Bickersteth.—The Great Dilemma. Christ His Own Witness or His Own Accuser. Six Lectures. Second Edition. Crown 8vo, 3s. 6d.

Our Public Schools—Eton, Harrow, Winchester, Rugby, Westminster, Marlborough, The Charterhouse. Crown 8vo, 6s.

OWEN, F. M.—John Keats : a Study. Crown 8vo, 6s.

Across the Hills. Small crown 8vo, 1s. 6d.

OWEN, Rev. Robert, B.D.—Sanctorale Catholicum ; or, Book of Saints. With Notes, Critical, Exegetical, and Historical. Demy 8vo, 18s.

OXENHAM, Rev. F. Nutcombe.—What is the Truth as to Everlasting Punishment. Part II. Being an Historical Inquiry into the Witness and Weight of certain Anti-Origenist Councils. Crown 8vo, 2s. 6d.

OXONIENSIS. — Romanism, Protestantism, Anglicanism. Being a Layman's View of some questions of the Day. Together with Remarks on Dr. Littledale's " Plain Reasons against joining the Church of Rome." Crown 8vo, 3s. 6d.

PALMER, the late William.—Notes of a Visit to Russia in 1840-1841. Selected and arranged by JOHN H. CARDINAL NEWMAN, with portrait. Crown 8vo, 8s. 6d.

Early Christian Symbolism. A Series of Compositions from Fresco Paintings, Glasses, and Sculptured Sarcophagi. Edited by the Rev. Provost NORTHCOTE, D.D., and the Rev. Canon BROWNLOW, M.A. In 8 Parts, each with 4 Plates. Folio, 5s. coloured ; 3s. plain.

Parchment Library. Choicely Printed on hand-made paper, limp parchment antique or cloth, 6s. ; vellum, 7s. 6d. each volume.

The Book of Psalms. Translated by the Rev. T. K. CHEYNE, M.A.

Parchment Library—*continued*.

The Vicar of Wakefield. With Preface and Notes by AUSTIN DOBSON.

English Comic Dramatists. Edited by OSWALD CRAWFURD.

English Lyrics.

The Sonnets of John Milton. Edited by MARK PATTISON. With Portrait after Vertue.

Poems by Alfred Tennyson. 2 vols. With miniature frontispieces by W. B. Richmond.

French Lyrics. Selected and Annotated by GEORGE SAINTSBURY. With a miniature frontispiece designed and etched by H. G. Glindoni.

Fables by Mr. John Gay. With Memoir by AUSTIN DOBSON, and an etched portrait from an unfinished Oil Sketch by Sir Godfrey Kneller.

Select Letters of Percy Bysshe Shelley. Edited, with an Introduction, by RICHARD GARNETT.

The Christian Year. Thoughts in Verse for the Sundays and Holy Days throughout the Year. With Miniature Portrait of the Rev. J. Keble, after a Drawing by G. Richmond, R.A.

Shakspere's Works. Complete in Twelve Volumes.

Eighteenth Century Essays. Selected and Edited by AUSTIN DOBSON. With a Miniature Frontispiece by R. Caldecott.

Q. Horati Flacci Opera. Edited by F. A. CORNISH, Assistant Master at Eton. With a Frontispiece after a design by L. Alma Tadema, etched by Leopold Lowenstam.

Edgar Allan Poe's Poems. With an Essay on his Poetry by ANDREW LANG, and a Frontispiece by Linley Sambourne.

* Shakspere's Sonnets. Edited by EDWARD DOWDEN. With a Frontispiece etched by Leopold Lowenstam, after the Death Mask.

English Odes. Selected by EDMUND W. GOSSE. With Frontispiece on India paper by Hamo Thornycroft, A.R.A.

Of the Imitation of Christ. By THOMAS À KEMPIS. A revised Translation. With Frontispiece on India paper, from a Design by W. B. Richmond.

Tennyson's The Princess: a Medley. With a Miniature Frontispiece by H. M. Paget, and a Tailpiece in Outline by Gordon Browne.

Poems: Selected from PERCY BYSSHE SHELLEY. Dedicated to Lady Shelley. With a Preface by RICHARD GARNETT and a Miniature Frontispiece.

Tennyson's In Memoriam. With a Miniature Portrait in *eau-forte* by Le Rat, after a Photograph by the late Mrs. Cameron.

*** The above volumes may also be had in a variety of leather bindings.

PARSLOE, Joseph.—Our Railways. Sketches, Historical and Descriptive. With Practical Information as to Fares and Rates, etc., and a Chapter on Railway Reform. Crown 8vo, 6s.

PAUL, Alexander.—Short Parliaments. A History of the National Demand for frequent General Elections. Small crown 8vo, 3s. 6d.

PAUL, C. Kegan.—Biographical Sketches, Printed on hand-made paper, bound in buckram. Second Edition. Crown 8vo, 7s. 6d.

PEARSON, Rev. S.—Week-day Living. A Book for Young Men and Women. Second Edition. Crown 8vo, 5s.

PESCHEL, Dr. Oscar.—The Races of Man and their Geographical Distribution. Second Edition. Large crown 8vo, 9s.

PETERS, F. H.—The Nicomachean Ethics of Aristotle. Translated by. Crown 8vo, 6s.

PHIPSON, E.—The Animal Lore of Shakspeare's Time. Including Quadrupeds, Birds, Reptiles, Fish and Insects. Large post 8vo, 9s.

PIDGEON, D.—An Engineer's Holiday ; or, Notes of a Round Trip from Long. 0° to 0°. New and Cheaper Edition. Large crown 8vo, 7s. 6d.

POPE, J. Buckingham. — Railway Rates and Radical Rule. Trade Questions as Election Tests. Crown 8vo, 2s. 6d.

PRICE, Prof. Bonamy. — Chapters on Practical Political Economy. Being the Substance of Lectures delivered before the University of Oxford. New and Cheaper Edition. Large post 8vo, 5s.

Pulpit Commentary, The. (Old Testament Series.) Edited by the Rev. J. S. EXELL, M.A., and the Rev. Canon H. D. M. SPENCE.

> Genesis. By the Rev. T. WHITELAW, M.A. With Homilies by the Very Rev. J. F. MONTGOMERY, D.D., Rev. Prof. R. A. REDFORD, M.A., LL.B., Rev. F. HASTINGS, Rev. W. ROBERTS, M.A. An Introduction to the Study of the Old Testament by the Venerable Archdeacon FARRAR, D.D., F.R.S. ; and Introductions to the Pentateuch by the Right Rev. H. COTTERILL, D.D., and Rev. T. WHITELAW, M.A. Eighth Edition. 1 vol., 15s.

> Exodus. By the Rev. Canon RAWLINSON. With Homilies by Rev. J. ORR, Rev. D. YOUNG, B.A., Rev. C. A. GOODHART, Rev. J. URQUHART, and the Rev. H. T. ROBJOHNS. Fourth Edition. 2 vols., 18s.

> Leviticus. By the Rev. Prebendary MEYRICK, M.A. With Introductions by the Rev. R. COLLINS, Rev. Professor A. CAVE, and Homilies by Rev. Prof. REDFORD, LL.B., Rev. J. A. MACDONALD, Rev. W. CLARKSON, B.A., Rev. S. R. ALDRIDGE, LL.B., and Rev. McCHEYNE EDGAR. Fourth Edition. 15s.

Pulpit Commentary, The—*continued.*

Numbers. By the Rev. R. WINTERBOTHAM, LL.B. With Homilies·by the Rev. Professor W. BINNIE, D.D., Rev. E. S. PROUT, M.A., Rev. D. YOUNG, Rev. J. WAITE, and an Introduction by the Rev. THOMAS WHITELAW, M.A. Fourth Edition. 15*s.*

Deuteronomy. By the Rev. W. L. ALEXANDER, D.D. With Homilies by Rev. C. CLEMANCE, D.D., Rev. J. ORR, B.D., Rev. R. M. EDGAR, M.A., Rev. D. DAVIES, M.A. Third edition. 15*s.*

Joshua. By Rev. J. J. LIAS, M.A. With Homilies by Rev. S. R. ALDRIDGE, LL.B., Rev. R. GLOVER, REV. E. DE PRESSENSÉ, D.D., Rev. J. WAITE, B.A., Rev. W. F. ADENEY, M.A. ; and an Introduction by the Rev. A. PLUMMER, M.A. Fifth Edition. 12*s.* 6*d.*

Judges and Ruth. By the Bishop of Bath and Wells, and Rev. J. MORRISON, D.D. With Homilies by Rev. A. F. MUIR, M.A., Rev. W. F. ADENEY, M.A., Rev. W. M. STATHAM, and Rev. Professor J. THOMSON, M.A. Fourth Edition. 10*s.* 6*d.*

1 Samuel. By the Very Rev. R. P. SMITH, D.D. With Homilies by Rev. DONALD FRASER, D.D., Rev. Prof. CHAPMAN, and Rev. B. DALE. Sixth Edition. 15*s.*

1 Kings. By the Rev. JOSEPH HAMMOND, LL.B. With Homilies by the Rev. E. DE PRESSENSÉ, D.D., Rev. J. WAITE, B.A., Rev. A. ROWLAND, LL.B., Rev. J. A. MACDONALD, and Rev. J. URQUHART. Fourth Edition. 15*s.*

Ezra, Nehemiah, and Esther. By Rev. Canon G. RAWLINSON, M.A. With Homilies by Rev. Prof. J. R. THOMSON, M.A., Rev. Prof. R. A. REDFORD, LL.B., M.A., Rev. W. S. LEWIS, M.A., Rev. J. A. MACDONALD, Rev. A. MACKENNAL, B.A., Rev. W. CLARKSON, B.A., Rev. F. HASTINGS, Rev. W. DINWIDDIE, LL.B., Rev. Prof. ROWLANDS, B.A., Rev. G. WOOD, B.A., Rev. Prof. P. C. BARKER, M.A., LL.B., and the Rev. J. S. EXELL, M.A. Sixth Edition. 1 vol., 12*s.* 6*d.*

Jeremiah. By the Rev. T. K. CHEYNE, M.A. With Homilies by the Rev. W. F. ADENEY, M.A., Rev. A. F. MUIR, M.A., Rev. S. CONWAY, B.A., Rev. J. WAITE, B.A., and Rev. D. YOUNG, B.A. Vol. I., 15s.

Pulpit Commentary, The. (New Testament Series.)

St. Mark. By Very Rev. E. BICKERSTETH, D.D., Dean of Lichfield. With Homilies by Rev. Prof. THOMSON, M.A., Rev. Prof. GIVEN, M.A., Rev. Prof. JOHNSON, M.A., Rev. A. ROWLAND, B.A., LL.B., Rev. A. MUIR, and Rev. R. GREEN. 2 vols. Fourth Edition. 21*s.*

The Acts of the Apostles. By the Bishop of Bath and Wells. With Homilies by Rev. Prof. P. C. BARKER, M.A., LL.B., Rev. Prof. E. JOHNSON, M.A., Rev. Prof. R. A. REDFORD, M.A., Rev. R. TUCK, B.A., Rev. W. CLARKSON, B.A. 2 vols., 21*s.*

Pulpit Commentary, The—*continued.*

    1 Corinthians. By the Ven. Archdeacon FARRAR, D.D. With Homilies by Rev. Ex-Chancellor LIPSCOMB, LL.D., Rev. DAVID THOMAS, D.D., Rev. D. FRASER, D.D., Rev. Prof. J. R. THOMSON, M.A., Rev. J. WAITE, B.A., Rev. R. TUCK, B.A., Rev. E. HURNDALL, M.A., and Rev. H. BREMNER, B.D. Price 15*s.*

PUSEY, Dr.—Sermons for the Church's Seasons from Advent to Trinity. Selected from the Published Sermons of the late EDWARD BOUVERIE PUSEY, D.D. Crown 8vo, 5*s.*

QUILTER, Harry.—"The Academy," 1872-1882. 1*s.*

RADCLIFFE, Frank R. Y.—The New Politicus. Small crown 8vo, 2*s. 6d.*

RANKE, Leopold von.—Universal History. The oldest Historical Group of Nations and the Greeks. Edited by G. W. PROTHERO. Demy 8vo, 16*s.*

Realities of the Future Life. Small crown 8vo, 1*s. 6d.*

RENDELL, J. M.—Concise Handbook of the Island of Madeira. With Plan of Funchal and Map of the Island. Fcap. 8vo, 1*s. 6d.*

REYNOLDS, Rev. J. W.—The Supernatural in Nature. A Verification by Free Use of Science. Third Edition, Revised and Enlarged. Demy 8vo, 14*s.*

The Mystery of Miracles. Third and Enlarged Edition. Crown 8vo, 6*s.*

The Mystery of the Universe; Our Common Faith. Demy 8vo, 14*s.*

RIBOT, Prof. Th.—Heredity: A Psychological Study on its Phenomena, its Laws, its Causes, and its Consequences. Second Edition. Large crown 8vo, 9*s.*

ROBERTSON, The late Rev. F. W., M.A.—Life and Letters of. Edited by the Rev. STOPFORD BROOKE, M.A.

    I. Two vols., uniform with the Sermons. With Steel Portrait. Crown 8vo, 7*s. 6d.*

    II. Library Edition, in Demy 8vo, with Portrait. 12*s.*

    III. A Popular Edition, in 1 vol. Crown 8vo, 6*s.*

Sermons. Four Series. Small crown 8vo, 3*s. 6d.* each.

The Human Race, and other Sermons. Preached at Cheltenham, Oxford, and Brighton. New and Cheaper Edition. Small crown 8vo, 3*s. 6d.*

Notes on Genesis. New and Cheaper Edition. Small crown 8vo, 3*s. 6d.*

Expository Lectures on St. Paul's Epistles to the Corinthians. A New Edition. Small crown 8vo, 5*s.*

Lectures and Addresses, with other Literary Remains. A New Edition. Small crown 8vo, 5*s.*

ROBERTSON, The late Rev. F. W., M.A.—continued.

An Analysis of Mr. Tennyson's "In Memoriam." (Dedicated by Permission to the Poet-Laureate.) Fcap. 8vo, 2s.

The Education of the Human Race. Translated from the German of GOTTHOLD EPHRAIM LESSING. Fcap. 8vo, 2s. 6d.

The above Works can also be had, bound in half morocco.

*** A Portrait of the late Rev. F. W. Robertson, mounted for framing, can be had, 2s. 6d.

ROMANES, G. J.—Mental Evolution in Animals. With a Posthumous Essay on Instinct by CHARLES DARWIN, F.R.S. Demy 8vo, 12s.

ROSMINI SERBATI, A., Founder of the Institute of Charity. Life. By G. STUART MACWALTER. 2 vols. 8vo.
[Vol. I. now ready, 12s.

Rosmini's Origin of Ideas. Translated from the Fifth Italian Edition of the Nuovo Saggio *Sull' origine delle idee.* 3 vols. Demy 8vo, cloth. [Vols. I. and II. now ready, 16s. each.

Rosmini's Philosophical System. Translated, with a Sketch of the Author's Life, Bibliography, Introduction, and Notes by THOMAS DAVIDSON. Demy 8vo, 16s.

RULE, Martin, M.A.—The Life and Times of St. Anselm, Archbishop of Canterbury and Primate of the Britains. 2 vols. Demy 8vo, 32s.

SALVATOR, Archduke Ludwig.—Levkosia, the Capital of Cyprus. Crown 4to, 10s. 6d.

SAMUEL, Sydney M.—Jewish Life in the East. Small crown 8vo, 3s. 6d.

SAYCE, Rev. Archibald Henry.—Introduction to the Science of Language. 2 vols. Second Edition. Large post 8vo, 21s.

Scientific Layman. The New Truth and the Old Faith : are they Incompatible ? Demy 8vo, 10s. 6d.

SCOONES, W. Baptiste.—Four Centuries of English Letters : A Selection of 350 Letters by 150 Writers, from the Period of the Paston Letters to the Present Time. Third Edition. Large crown 8vo, 6s.

SHILLITO, Rev. Joseph.—Womanhood : its Duties, Temptations, and Privileges. A Book for Young Women. Third Edition. Crown 8vo, 3s. 6d.

SHIPLEY, Rev. Orby, M.A.—Principles of the Faith in Relation to Sin. Topics for Thought in Times of Retreat. Eleven Addresses delivered during a Retreat of Three Days to Persons living in the World. Demy 8vo, 12s.

Sister Augustine, Superior of the Sisters of Charity at the St. Johannis Hospital at Bonn. Authorised Translation by HANS THARAU, from the German "Memorials of AMALIE VON LASAULX." Cheap Edition. Large crown 8vo, 4s. 6d.

SKINNER, James.—A Memoir. By the Author of "Charles Lowder." With a Preface by the Rev. Canon CARTER, and Portrait. Large crown, 7s. 6d.

SMITH, Edward, M.D., LL.B., F.R.S.—Tubercular Consumption in its Early and Remediable Stages. Second Edition. Crown 8vo, 6s.

SPEDDING, James.—Reviews and Discussions, Literary, Political, and Historical not relating to Bacon. Demy 8vo, 12s. 6d.

Evenings with a Reviewer; or, Bacon and Macaulay. With a Prefatory Notice by G. S. VENABLES, Q.C. 2 vols. Demy 8vo, 18s.

STAPFER, Paul.—Shakspeare and Classical Antiquity: Greek and Latin Antiquity as presented in Shakspeare's Plays. Translated by EMILY J. CAREY. Large post 8vo, 12s.

STEVENSON, Rev. W. F.—Hymns for the Church and Home. Selected and Edited by the Rev. W. FLEMING STEVENSON. The Hymn Book consists of Three Parts:—I. For Public Worship.—II. For Family and Private Worship.—III. For Children.
*** Published in various forms and prices, the latter ranging from 8d. to 6s.

Stray Papers on Education, and Scenes from School Life. By B. H. Second Edition. Small crown 8vo, 3s. 6d.

STREATFEILD, Rev. G. S., M.A.—Lincolnshire and the Danes. Large crown 8vo, 7s. 6d.

STRECKER-WISLICENUS.—Organic Chemistry. Translated and Edited, with Extensive Additions, by W. R. HODGKINSON, Ph.D., and A. J. GREENAWAY, F.I.C. Demy 8vo, 21s.

Study of the Prologue and Epilogue in English Literature. From Shakespeare to Dryden. By G. S. B. Crown 8vo, 5s.

SULLY, James, M.A.—Pessimism: a History and a Criticism. Second Edition. Demy 8vo, 14s.

SWEDENBORG, Eman.—De Cultu et Amore Dei ubi Agitur de Telluris ortu, Paradiso et Vivario, tum de Primogeniti Seu Adami Nativitate Infantia, et Amore. Crown 8vo, 6s.

SYME, David.—Representative Government in England. Its Faults and Failures. Second Edition. Large crown 8vo, 6s.

TAYLOR, Rev. Isaac.—The Alphabet. An Account of the Origin and Development of Letters. With numerous Tables and Facsimiles. 2 vols. Demy 8vo, 36s.

TAYLOR, Sedley. — Profit Sharing between Capital and Labour. To which is added a Memorandum on the Industrial Partnership at the Whitwood Collieries, by ARCHIBALD and HENRY BRIGGS, with remarks by SEDLEY TAYLOR. Crown 8vo, 2s. 6d.

Thirty Thousand Thoughts. Edited by the Rev. CANON SPENCE, Rev. J. S. EXELL, Rev. CHARLES NEIL, and Rev. JACOB STEPHENSON. 6 vols. Super royal 8vo.
[Vols. I. and II. now ready, 16s. each.

THOM, J. Hamilton.—Laws of Life after the Mind of Christ. Second Edition. Crown 8vo, 7s. 6d.

THOMSON, J. Turnbull.—Social Problems; or, An Inquiry into the Laws of Influence. With Diagrams. Demy 8vo, 10s. 6d.

TIDMAN, Paul F.—Gold and Silver Money. Part I.—A Plain Statement. Part II.—Objections Answered. Third Edition. Crown 8vo, 1s.

TIPPLE, Rev. S. A.—Sunday Mornings at Norwood. Prayers and Sermons. Crown 8vo, 6s.

TODHUNTER, Dr. J.—A Study of Shelley. Crown 8vo, 7s.

TREMENHEERE, Hugh Seymour, C.B.— A Manual of the Principles of Government, as set forth by the Authorities of Ancient and Modern Times. New and Enlarged Edition. Crown 8vo, 3s. 6d.

TUKE, Daniel Hack, M.D., F.R.C.P.--Chapters in the History of the Insane in the British Isles. With 4 Illustrations. Large crown 8vo, 12s.

TWINING, Louisa.—Workhouse Visiting and Management during Twenty-Five Years. Small crown 8vo, 2s.

TYLER, J.—The Mystery of Being: or, What Do We Know? Small crown 8vo, 3s. 6d.

UPTON, Major R. D.—Gleanings from the Desert of Arabia. Large post 8vo, 10s. 6d.

VACUUS VIATOR.—Flying South. Recollections of France and its Littoral. Small crown 8vo, 3s. 6d.

VAUGHAN, H. Halford.—New Readings and Renderings of Shakespeare's Tragedies. 2 vols. Demy 8vo, 25s.

VILLARI, Professor.—Niccolò Machiavelli and his Times. Translated by Linda Villari. 4 vols. Large post 8vo, 48s.

VILLIERS, The Right Hon. C. P.—Free Trade Speeches of. With Political Memoir. Edited by a Member of the Cobden Club. 2 vols. With Portrait. Demy 8vo, 25s.
₊ People's Edition. 1 vol. Crown 8vo, limp cloth, 2s. 6d.

VOGT, Lieut.-Col. Hermann.—The Egyptian War of 1882. A translation. With Map and Plans. Large crown 8vo, 6s.

VOLCKXSOM, E. W. v.—Catechism of Elementary Modern Chemistry. Small crown 8vo, 3*s*.

VYNER, Lady Mary.—Every Day a Portion. Adapted from the Bible and the Prayer Book, for the Private Devotion of those living in Widowhood. Collected and Edited by Lady Mary Vyner. Square crown 8vo, 5*s*.

WALDSTEIN, Charles, Ph.D.—The Balance of Emotion and Intellect; an Introductory Essay to the Study of Philosophy. Crown 8vo, 6*s*.

WALLER, Rev. C. B.—The Apocalypse, reviewed under the Light of the Doctrine of the Unfolding Ages, and the Restitution of All Things. Demy 8vo, 12*s*.

VALPOLE, Chas. George.—History of Ireland from the Earliest Times to the Union with Great Britain. With 5 Maps and Appendices. Crown 8vo, 10*s. 6d.*

VALSHE, Walter Hayle, M.D.—Dramatic Singing Physiologically Estimated. Crown 8vo, 3*s. 6d.*

VARD, William George, Ph.D.—Essays on the Philosophy of Theism. Edited, with an Introduction, by WILFRID WARD. 2 vols. Demy 8vo, 21*s*.

VEDDERBURN, Sir David, Bart., M.P.—Life of. Compiled from his Journals and Writings by his sister, Mrs. E. H. PERCIVAL. With etched Portrait, and facsimiles of Pencil Sketches. Demy 8vo, 14*s*.

VEDMORE, Frederick.—The Masters of Genre Painting. With Sixteen Illustrations. Post 8vo, 7*s. 6d.*

VHEWELL, William, D.D.—His Life and Selections from his Correspondence. By Mrs. STAIR DOUGLAS. With a Portrait from a Painting by Samuel Laurence. Demy 8vo, 21*s*.

VHITNEY, Prof. William Dwight.—Essentials of English Grammar, for the Use of Schools. Second Edition. Crown 8vo, 3*s. 6d.*

VILLIAMS, Rowland, D.D.—Psalms, Litanies, Counsels, and Collects for Devout Persons. Edited by his Widow. New and Popular Edition. Crown 8vo, 3*s. 6d.*

Stray Thoughts Collected from the Writings of the late Rowland Williams, D.D. Edited by his Widow. Crown 8vo, 3*s. 6d.*

VILSON, Sir Erasmus. — The Recent Archaic Discovery of Egyptian Mummies at Thebes. A Lecture. Crown 8vo, 1*s. 6d.*

VILSON, Lieut -Col. C. T. — The Duke of Berwick, Marshal of France, 1702–1734. Demy 8vo, 15*s*.

VILSON, Mrs. R. F.—The Christian Brothers. Their Origin and Work. With a Sketch of the Life of their Founder, the Ven. JEAN BAPTISTE, de la Salle. Crown 8vo, 6*s*.

WOLTMANN, Dr. Alfred, and WOERMANN, Dr. Karl.—History of Painting. Edited by SIDNEY COLVIN. Vol. I. Painting in Antiquity and the Middle Ages. With numerous Illustrations. Medium 8vo, 28*s.* ; bevelled boards, gilt leaves, 30*s.*

Word was Made Flesh. Short Family Readings on the Epistles for each Sunday of the Christian Year. Demy 8vo, 10*s.* 6*d.*

WREN, Sir Christopher.—**His Family and His Times.** With Original Letters, and a Discourse on Architecture hitherto unpublished. By LUCY PHILLIMORE. Demy 8vo, 10*s.* 6*d.*

YOUMANS, Eliza A.—**First Book of Botany.** Designed to Cultivate the Observing Powers of Children. With 300 Engravings. New and Cheaper Edition. Crown 8vo, 2*s.* 6*d.*

YOUMANS, Edward L., M.D.—**A Class Book of Chemistry,** on the Basis of the New System. With 200 Illustrations. Crown 8vo, 5*s.*

THE INTERNATIONAL SCIENTIFIC SERIES.

I. **Forms of Water:** a Familiar Exposition of the Origin and Phenomena of Glaciers. By J. Tyndall, LL.D., F.R.S. With 25 Illustrations. Eighth Edition. Crown 8vo, 5*s.*

II. **Physics and Politics ;** or, Thoughts on the Application of the Principles of "Natural Selection" and "Inheritance" to Political Society. By Walter Bagehot. Sixth Edition. Crown 8vo, 4*s.*

III. **Foods.** By Edward Smith, M.D., LL.B., F.R.S. With numerous Illustrations. Eighth Edition. Crown 8vo, 5*s.*

IV. **Mind and Body:** the Theories of their Relation. By Alexander Bain, LL.D. With Four Illustrations. Seventh Edition. Crown 8vo, 4*s.*

V. **The Study of Sociology.** By Herbert Spencer. Eleventh Edition. Crown 8vo, 5*s.*

VI. **On the Conservation of Energy.** By Balfour Stewart, M.A., LL.D., F.R.S. With 14 Illustrations. Sixth Edition. Crown 8vo, 5*s.*

VII. **Animal Locomotion ;** or Walking, Swimming, and Flying. By J. B. Pettigrew, M.D., F.R.S., etc. With 130 Illustrations. Third Edition. Crown 8vo, 5*s.*

VIII. **Responsibility in Mental Disease.** By Henry Maudsley, M.D. Fourth Edition. Crown 8vo, 5*s.*

IX. **The New Chemistry.** By Professor J. P. Cooke. With 31 Illustrations. Seventh Edition. Crown 8vo, 5*s.*

. **The Science of Law.** By Professor Sheldon Amos. Fifth Edition. Crown 8vo, 5*s.*

I. **Animal Mechanism :** a Treatise on Terrestrial and Aerial Loco-motion. By Professor E. J. Marey. With 117 Illustrations. Third Edition. Crown 8vo, 5*s.*

II. **The Doctrine of Descent and Darwinism.** By Professor Oscar Schmidt. With 26 Illustrations. Fifth Edition. Crown 8vo, 5*s.*

III. **The History of the Conflict between Religion and Science.** By J. W. Draper, M.D., LL.D. Eighteenth Edition. Crown 8vo, 5*s.*

IV. **Fungi :** their Nature, Influences, Uses, etc. By M. C. Cooke, M.D., LL.D. Edited by the Rev. M. J. Berkeley, M.A., F.L.S. With numerous Illustrations. Third Edition. Crown 8vo, 5*s.*

V. **The Chemical Effects of Light and Photography.** By Dr. Hermann Vogel. Translation thoroughly Revised. With 100 Illustrations. Fourth Edition. Crown 8vo, 5*s.*

VI. **The Life and Growth of Language.** By Professor William Dwight Whitney. Fourth Edition. Crown 8vo, 5*s.*

VII. **Money and the Mechanism of Exchange.** By W. Stanley Jevons, M.A., F.R.S. Sixth Edition. Crown 8vo, 5*s.*

VIII. **The Nature of Light.** With a General Account of Physical Optics. By Dr. Eugene Lommel. With 188 Illustrations and a Table of Spectra in Chromo-lithography. Third Edition. Crown 8vo, 5*s.*

IX. **Animal Parasites and Messmates.** By Monsieur Van Beneden. With 83 Illustrations. Third Edition. Crown 8vo, 5*s.*

X. **Fermentation.** By Professor Schützenberger. With 28 Illus-trations. Fourth Edition. Crown 8vo, 5*s.*

XI: **The Five Senses of Man.** By Professor Bernstein. With 91 Illustrations. Fourth Edition. Crown 8vo, 5*s.*

XII. **The Theory of Sound in its Relation to Music.** By Pro-fessor Pietro Blaserna. With numerous Illustrations. Third Edition. Crown 8vo, 5*s.*

XIII. **Studies in Spectrum Analysis.** By J. Norman Lockyer, F.R.S. With six photographic Illustrations of Spectra, and numerous engravings on Wood. Third Edition. Crown 8vo, 6*s.* 6*d.*

XIV. **A History of the Growth of the Steam Engine.** By Professor R. H. Thurston. With numerous Illustrations. Third Edition. Crown 8vo, 6*s.* 6*d.*

XV. **Education as a Science.** By Alexander Bain, LL.D. Fourth Edition. Crown 8vo, 5*s.*

XXVI. **The Human Species.** By Professor A. de Quatrefages. Third Edition. Crown 8vo, 5*s*.

XXVII. **Modern Chromatics.** With Applications to Art and Industry. By Ogden N. Rood. With 130 original Illustrations. Second Edition. Crown 8vo, 5*s*.

XXVIII. **The Crayfish :** an Introduction to the Study of Zoology. By Professor T. H. Huxley. With 82 Illustrations. Third Edition. Crown 8vo, 5*s*.

XXIX. **The Brain as an Organ of Mind.** By H. Charlton Bastian, M.D. With numerous Illustrations. Third Edition. Crown 8vo, 5*s*.

XXX. **The Atomic Theory.** By Prof. Wurtz. Translated by G. Cleminshaw, F.C.S. Third Edition. Crown 8vo, 5*s*.

XXXI. **The Natural Conditions of Existence as they affect Animal Life.** By Karl Semper. With 2 Maps and 106 Woodcuts. Third Edition. Crown 8vo, 5*s*.

XXXII. **General Physiology of Muscles and Nerves.** By Prof. J. Rosenthal. Third Edition. With Illustrations. Crown 8vo, 5*s*.

XXXIII. **Sight :** an Exposition of the Principles of Monocular and Binocular Vision. By Joseph le Conte, LL.D. Second Edition. With 132 Illustrations. Crown 8vo, 5*s*.

XXXIV. **Illusions :** a Psychological Study. By James Sully. Second Edition. Crown 8vo, 5*s*.

XXXV. **Volcanoes : what they are and what they teach.** By Professor J. W. Judd, F.R.S. With 92 Illustrations on Wood. Second Edition. Crown 8vo, 5*s*.

XXXVI. **Suicide :** an Essay in Comparative Moral Statistics. By Prof. E. Morselli. Second Edition. With Diagrams. Crown 8vo, 5*s*.

XXXVII. **The Brain and its Functions.** By J. Luys. With Illustrations. Second Edition. Crown 8vo, 5*s*.

XXXVIII. **Myth and Science :** an Essay. By Tito Vignoli. Second Edition. Crown 8vo, 5*s*.

XXXIX. **The Sun.** By Professor Young. With Illustrations. Second Edition. Crown 8vo, 5*s*.

XL. **Ants, Bees, and Wasps :** a Record of Observations on the Habits of the Social Hymenoptera. By Sir John Lubbock, Bart., M.P. With 5 Chromo-lithographic Illustrations. Sixth Edition. Crown 8vo, 5*s*.

XLI. **Animal Intelligence.** By G. J. Romanes, LL.D., F.R.S. Third Edition. Crown 8vo, 5*s*.

XLII. **The Concepts and Theories of Modern Physics.** By J. B. Stallo. Second Edition. Crown 8vo, 5s.

XLIII. **Diseases of the Memory**; An Essay in the Positive Psychology. By Prof. Th. Ribot. Second Edition. Crown 8vo, 5s.

XLIV. **Man before Metals.** By N. Joly, with 148 Illustrations. Third Edition. Crown 8vo, 5s.

XLV. **The Science of Politics.** By Prof. Sheldon Amos. Second Edition. Crown 8vo, 5s.

XLVI. **Elementary Meteorology.** By Robert H. Scott. Second Edition. With Numerous Illustrations. Crown 8vo, 5s.

XLVII. **The Organs of Speech and their Application in the Formation of Articulate Sounds.** By Georg Hermann Von Meyer. With 47 Woodcuts. Crown 8vo, 5s.

XLVIII. **Fallacies.** A View of Logic from the Practical Side. By Alfred Sidgwick. Crown 8vo, 5s.

MILITARY WORKS.

BARRINGTON, Capt. J. T.—**England on the Defensive**; or, the Problem of Invasion Critically Examined. Large crown 8vo, with Map, 7s. 6d.

BRACKENBURY, Col. C. B., R.A.—**Military Handbooks for Regimental Officers.**

I. **Military Sketching and Reconnaissance.** By Col. F. J. Hutchison and Major H. G. MacGregor. Fourth Edition. With 15 Plates. Small crown 8vo, 4s.

II. **The Elements of Modern Tactics Practically applied to English Formations.** By Lieut.-Col. Wilkinson Shaw. Fourth Edition. With 25 Plates and Maps. Small crown 8vo, 9s.

III. **Field Artillery.** Its Equipment, Organization and Tactics. By Major Sisson C. Pratt, R.A. With 12 Plates. Second Edition. Small crown 8vo, 6s.

IV. **The Elements of Military Administration.** First Part: Permanent System of Administration. By Major J. W. Buxton. Small crown 8vo. 7s. 6d.

V. **Military Law**: Its Procedure and Practice. By Major Sisson C. Pratt, R.A. Second Edition. Small crown 8vo, 4s. 6d.

BROOKE, Major, C. K.—**A System of Field Training.** Small crown 8vo, cloth limp, 2s.

CLERY, C., Lieut.-Col.—**Minor Tactics.** With 26 Maps and Plans. Sixth and Cheaper Edition, Revised. Crown 8vo, 9s.

COLVILE, Lieut.-Col. C. F.—**Military Tribunals.** Sewed, 2s. 6d.

CRAUFURD, Lieut. H.J.—**Suggestions for the Military Training of a Company of Infantry.** Crown 8vo, 1s. 6d.

HARRISON, Lieut.-Col. R.—**The Officer's Memorandum Book for Peace and War.** Third Edition. Oblong 32mo, roan, with pencil, 3s. 6d.

Notes on Cavalry Tactics, Organisation, etc. By a Cavalry Officer. With Diagrams. Demy 8vo, 12s.

PARR, Capt. H. Hallam, C.M.G.—**The Dress, Horses, and Equipment of Infantry and Staff Officers.** Crown 8vo, 1s.

SCHAW, Col. H.—**The Defence and Attack of Positions and Localities.** Second Edition, Revised and Corrected. Crown 8vo, 3s. 6d.

SHADWELL, Maj.-Gen., C.B.—**Mountain Warfare.** Illustrated by the Campaign of 1799 in Switzerland. Being a Translation of the Swiss Narrative compiled from the Works of the Archduke Charles, Jomini, and others. Also of Notes by General H. Dufour on the Campaign of the Valtelline in 1635. With Appendix, Maps, and Introductory Remarks. Demy 8vo, 16s.

WILKINSON, H. Spenser, Capt. 20th Lancashire R.V.—**Citizen Soldiers.** Essays towards the Improvement of the Volunteer Force. Crown 8vo, 2s. 6d.

POETRY.

ADAM OF ST. VICTOR.—**The Liturgical Poetry of Adam of St. Victor.** From the text of GAUTIER. With Translations into English in the Original Metres, and Short Explanatory Notes, by DIGBY S. WRANGHAM, M.A. 3 vols. Crown 8vo, printed on hand-made paper, boards, 21s.

AUCHMUTY, A. C.—**Poems of English Heroism :** From Brunanburh to Lucknow ; from Athelstan to Albert. Small crown 8vo, 1s. 6d.

AVIA.—**The Odyssey of Homer.** Done into English Verse by. Fcap. 4to, 15s.

BANKS, Mrs. G. L.—**Ripples and Breakers :** Poems. Square 8vo, 5s.

BARING, T. C., M.A., M.P. — **The Scheme of Epicurus.** A Rendering into English Verse of the Unfinished Poem of Lucretius, entitled " De Rerum Naturâ " ("The Nature of Things"). Fcap. 4to.

BARNES, William.—Poems of Rural Life, in the Dorset Dialect. New Edition, complete in one vol. Crown 8vo, 8s. 6d.

BAYNES, Rev. Canon H. R.—Home Songs for Quiet Hours. Fourth and Cheaper Edition. Fcap. 8vo, cloth, 2s. 6d.
*** This may also be had handsomely bound in morocco with gilt edges.

BENDALL, Gerard.—Musa Silvestris. 16mo, 1s. 6d.

BEVINGTON, L. S.—Key Notes. Small crown 8vo, 5s.

BILLSON, C. J.—The Acharnians of Aristophanes. Crown 8vo, 3s. 6d.

BLUNT, Wilfrid Scawen. — The Wind and the Whirlwind. Demy 8vo, 1s. 6d.

BOWEN, H. C., M.A.—Simple English Poems. English Literature for Junior Classes. In Four Parts. Parts I., II., and III., 6d. each, and Part IV., 1s. Complete, 3s.

BRASHER, Alfred.—Sophia ; or, the Viceroy of Valencia. A Comedy in Five Acts, founded on a Story in Scarron. Small crown 8vo, 2s. 6d.

BRYANT, W. C.—Poems. Cheap Edition, with Frontispiece. Small crown 8vo, 3s. 6d.

BYRNNE, E. Fairfax.—Milicent : a Poem. Small crown 8vo, 6s.

CAILLARD, Emma Marie.—Charlotte Corday, and other Poems. Small crown 8vo, 3s. 6d.

Calderon's Dramas : the Wonder-Working Magician — Life is a Dream—the Purgatory of St. Patrick. Translated by DENIS FLORENCE MACCARTHY. Post 8vo, 10s.

Camoens Lusiads. -- Portuguese Text, with Translation by J. J. AUBERTIN. Second Edition. 2 vols. Crown 8vo, 12s.

CAMPBELL, Lewis.—Sophocles. The Seven Plays in English Verse. Crown 8vo, 7s. 6d.

Castilian Brothers (The), Chateaubriant, Waldemar : Three Tragedies ; and The Rose of Sicily : a Drama. By the Author of "Ginevra," etc. Crown 8vo, 6s.

Chronicles of Christopher Columbus. A Poem in 12 Cantos. By M. D. C. Crown 8vo, 7s. 6d.

CLARKE, Mary Cowden. — Honey from the Weed. Verses. Crown 8vo, 7s.

Cosmo de Medici ; The False One ; Agramont and Beaumont : Three Tragedies ; and The Deformed : a Dramatic Sketch. By the Author of "Ginevra," etc., etc. Crown 8vo, 5s.

D

COXHEAD, Ethel.—**Birds and Babies.** Imp. 16mo. With 33 Illustrations. Gilt, 2s. 6d.

David Rizzio, Bothwell, and the Witch Lady: Three Tragedies. By the author of " Ginevra," etc. Crown 8vo, 6s.

DAVIE, G. S., M.D.—**The Garden of Fragrance.** Being a complete translation of the Bostán of Sádi from the original Persian into English Verse. Crown 8vo, 7s. 6d.

DAVIES, T. Hart.—**Catullus.** Translated into English Verse. Crown 8vo, 6s.

DENNIS, J.—**English Sonnets.** Collected and Arranged by. Small crown 8vo, 2s. 6d.

DE VERE, Aubrey.—**Poetical Works.**

    I. THE SEARCH AFTER PROSERPINE, etc. 6s.
    II. THE LEGENDS OF ST. PATRICK, etc. 6s.
    III. ALEXANDER THE GREAT, etc. 6s.

    The Foray of Queen Meave, and other Legends of Ireland's Heroic Age. Small crown 8vo, 5s.

    Legends of the Saxon Saints. Small crown 8vo, 6s.

DILLON, Arthur.—**River Songs and other Poems.** With 13 autotype Illustrations from designs by Margery May. Fcap. 4to, cloth extra, gilt leaves, 10s. 6d.

DOBELL, Mrs. Horace.—**Ethelstone, Eveline,** and other Poems. Crown 8vo, 6s.

DOBSON, Austin.—**Old World Idylls** and other Poems. Third Edition. 18mo, cloth extra, gilt tops, 6s.

DOMET, Alfred.—**Ranolf and Amohia.** A Dream of Two Lives. New Edition, Revised. 2 vols. Crown 8vo, 12s.

Dorothy: a Country Story in Elegiac Verse. With Preface. Demy 8vo, 5s.

DOWDEN, Edward, LL.D.—**Shakspere's Sonnets.** With Introduction and Notes. Large post 8vo, 7s. 6d.

DUTT, Toru.—**A Sheaf Gleaned in French Fields.** New Edition. Demy 8vo, 10s. 6d.

EDMONDS, E. W.—**Hesperas.** Rhythm and Rhyme. Crown 8vo, 4s.

ELDRYTH, Maud.—**Margaret,** and other Poems. Small crown 8vo, 3s. 6d.

    All Soul's Eve, " No God," and other Poems. Fcap. 8vo, 3s. 6d.

ELLIOTT, Ebenezer, The Corn Law Rhymer.—**Poems.** Edited by his son, the Rev. EDWIN ELLIOTT, of St. John's, Antigua. 2 vols. Crown 8vo, 18s.

English Odes. Selected, with a Critical Introduction by EDMUND W. GOSSE, and a miniature frontispiece by Hamo Thornycroft, A.R.A. Elzevir 8vo, limp parchment antique, or cloth, 6s. ; vellum, 7s. 6d.

English Verse. Edited by W. J. LINTON and R. H. STODDARD. 5 vols. Crown 8vo, cloth, 5s. each.
  I. CHAUCER TO BURNS.
  II. TRANSLATIONS.
  III. LYRICS OF THE NINETEENTH CENTURY.
  IV. DRAMATIC SCENES AND CHARACTERS.
  V. BALLADS AND ROMANCES.

EVANS, Anne.—**Poems and Music.** With Memorial Preface by ANN THACKERAY RITCHIE. Large crown 8vo, 7s.

GOSSE, Edmund W.—**New Poems.** Crown 8vo, 7s. 6d.

GRAHAM, William. **Two Fancies, and other Poems.** Crown 8vo, 5s.

GRINDROD, Charles. **Plays from English History.** Crown 8vo, 7s. 6d.

  The Stranger's Story, and his Poem, The Lament of Love: An Episode of the Malvern Hills. Small crown 8vo, 2s. 6d.

GURNEY, Rev. Alfred.—**The Vision of the Eucharist,** and other Poems. Crown 8vo, 5s.

HELLON, H. G.—**Daphnis:** a Pastoral Poem. Small crown 8vo, 3s. 6d.

HENRY, Daniel, Junr.—**Under a Fool's Cap.** Songs. Crown 8vo, cloth, bevelled boards, 5s.

Herman Waldgrave: a Life's Drama. By the Author of "Ginevra," etc. Crown 8vo, 6s.

HICKEY, E. H.—**A Sculptor,** and other Poems. Small crown 8vo, 5s.

HONEYWOOD, Patty.—**Poems.** Dedicated (by permission) to Lord Wolseley, G.C.B., etc. Small crown 8vo, 2s. 6d.

INGHAM, Sarson, C. J.—**Cædmon's Vision, and other Poems.** Small crown 8vo, 5s.

JENKINS, Rev. Canon.—**Alfonso Petrucci,** Cardinal and Conspirator: an Historical Tragedy in Five Acts. Small crown 8vo, 3s. 6d.

JOHNSON, Ernle S. W.—**Ilaria,** and other Poems. Small crown 8vo, 3s. 6d.

KEATS, John.—**Poetical Works.** Edited by W. T. ARNOLD. Large crown 8vo, choicely printed on hand-made paper, with Portrait in *eau-forte.* Parchment, 12s.; vellum, 15s.

KING, Edward.—**Echoes from the Orient.** With Miscellaneous Poems. Small crown 8vo, 3s. 6d.

KING, Mrs. Hamilton.—**The Disciples.** Sixth Edition, with Portrait and Notes. Crown 8vo, 5s.

  A Book of Dreams. Crown 8vo, 3s. 6d.

KNOX, The Hon. Mrs. O. N.—**Four Pictures from a Life,** and other Poems. Small crown 8vo, 3s. 6d.

LANG, A.—**XXXII** Ballades in Blue China. Elzevir 8vo, parchment, 5*s*.

LAWSON, Right Hon. Mr. Justice.—Hymni Usitati Latine Redditi : with other Verses. Small 8vo, parchment, 5*s*.

Lessings Nathan the Wise. Translated by EUSTACE K. CORBETT. Crown 8vo, 6*s*.

Life Thoughts. Small crown 8vo, 2*s*. 6*d*.

Living English Poets MDCCCLXXXII. With Frontispiece by Walter Crane. Second Edition. Large crown 8vo. Printed on hand-made paper. Parchment, 12*s*. ; vellum, 15*s*.

LOCKER, F.—London Lyrics. A New and Cheaper Edition. Small crown 8vo, 2*s*. 6*d*.

Love in Idleness. A Volume of Poems. With an etching by W. B. Scott. Small crown 8vo, 5*s*.

Love Sonnets of Proteus. With Frontispiece by the Author. Elzevir 8vo, 5*s*.

LUMSDEN, Lieut.-Col. H. W.—Beowulf : an Old English Poem. Translated into Modern Rhymes. Second and Revised Edition. Small crown 8vo, 5*s*.

Lyre and Star. Poems by the Author of " Ginevra," etc. Crown 8vo, 5*s*.

MAGNUSSON, Eirikr, M.A., and PALMER, E. H., M.A.—Johan Ludvig Runeberg's Lyrical Songs, Idylls, and Epigrams. Fcap. 8vo, 5*s*.

M.D.C.—Chronicles of Christopher Columbus. A Poem in Twelve Cantos. Crown 8vo, 7*s*. 6*d*.

MEREDITH, Owen [The Earl of Lytton].—Lucile. New Edition. With 32 Illustrations. 16mo, 3*s*. 6*d*. Cloth extra, gilt edges, 4*s*. 6*d*.

MORRIS, Lewis.—Poetical Works of. New and Cheaper Editions, with Portrait. Complete in 3 vols., 5*s*. each.

> Vol. I. contains " Songs of Two Worlds." Ninth Edition. Vol. II. contains " The Epic of Hades." Seventeenth Edition. Vol. III. contains " Gwen " and " The Ode of Life." Fifth Edition.

> The Epic of Hades. With 16 Autotype Illustrations, after the Drawings of the late George R. Chapman. 4to, cloth extra, gilt leaves, 21*s*.

> The Epic of Hades. Presentation Edition. 4to, cloth extra, gilt leaves, 10*s*. 6*d*.

> Songs Unsung. Fourth Edition. Fcap. 8vo, 6*s*.

MORSHEAD, E. D. A. — The House of Atreus. Being the Agamemnon, Libation-Bearers, and Furies of Æschylus. Translated into English Verse. Crown 8vo, 7*s*.

> The Suppliant Maidens of Æschylus. Crown 8vo, 3*s*. 6*d*.

NADEN, Constance W.—Songs and Sonnets of Spring Time. Small crown 8vo, 5s.

NEWELL, E. J.—The Sorrows of Simona and Lyrical Verses. Small crown 8vo, 3s. 6d.

NOEL, The Hon. Roden. — A Little Child's Monument. Third Edition. Small crown 8vo, 3s. 6d.

    The Red Flag, and other Poems. New Edition. Small crown 8vo, 6s.

O'HAGAN, John.—The Song of Roland. Translated into English Verse. New and Cheaper Edition. Crown 8vo, 5s.

PFEIFFER, Emily.—The Rhyme of the Lady of the Lock, and How it Grew. Small crown 8vo, 3s. 6d.

    Gerard's Monument, and other Poems. Second Edition. Crown 8vo, 6s.

    Under the Aspens: Lyrical and Dramatic. With Portrait. Crown 8vo, 6s.

PIATT, J. J.—Idyls and Lyrics of the Ohio Valley. Crown 8vo, 5s.

POE, Edgar Allan.—Poems. With an Essay on his Poetry by ANDREW LANG, and a Frontispiece by Linley Sambourne. Parchment Library Edition.—Parchment or cloth, 6s. ; vellum, 7s. 6d.

RAFFALOVICH, Mark André. — Cyril and Lionel, and other Poems. A volume of Sentimental Studies. Small crown 8vo, 3s. 6d.

Rare Poems of the 16th and 17th Centuries. Edited W. J. LINTON. Crown 8vo, 5s.

RHOADES, James.—The Georgics of Virgil. Translated into English Verse. Small crown 8vo, 5s.

ROBINSON, A. Mary F.—A Handful of Honeysuckle. Fcap. 8vo, 3s. 6d.

    The Crowned Hippolytus. Translated from Euripides. With New Poems. Small crown 8vo, 5s.

Schiller's Mary Stuart. German Text, with English Translation on opposite page by LEEDHAM WHITE. Crown 8vo, 6s.

SCOTT, George F. E.—Theodora and other Poems. Small crown 8vo, 3s. 6d.

SEAL, W. H.—Ione, and other Poems. Crown 8vo, gilt tops, 5s.

SELKIRK, J. B.—Poems. Crown 8vo, 7s. 6d.

Shakspere's Sonnets. Edited by EDWARD DOWDEN. With a Frontispiece etched by Leopold Lowenstam, after the Death Mask. Parchment Library Edition.—Parchment or cloth, 6s. ; vellum, 7s. 6d.

Shakspere's Works. Complete in 12 Volumes. Parchment Library Edition.—Parchment or cloth, 6s. each; vellum, 7s. 6d. each.

SHAW, W. F., M.A.—**Juvenal, Persius, Martial, and Catullus.** An Experiment in Translation. Crown 8vo, 5s.

SHELLEY, Percy Bysshe.—**Poems Selected from.** Dedicated to Lady Shelley. With Preface by RICHARD GARNETT. Parchment Library Edition.—Parchment or cloth, 6s.; vellum, 7s. 6d.

Six Ballads about King Arthur. Crown 8vo, cloth extra, gilt edges, 3s. 6d.

SKINNER, H. J.—**The Lily of the Lyn,** and other Poems. Small crown 8vo, 3s. 6d.

SLADEN, Douglas B.—**Frithjof and Ingebjorg,** and other Poems. Small crown 8vo, 5s.

SMITH, J. W. Gilbart.—**The Loves of Vandyck.** A Tale of Genoa. Small crown 8vo, 2s. 6d.

Sophocles : The Seven Plays in English Verse. Translated by LEWIS CAMPBELL. Crown 8vo, 7s. 6d.

SPICER, Henry.—**Haska :** a Drama in Three Acts (as represented at the Theatre Royal, Drury Lane, March 10th, 1877). Third Edition. Crown 8vo, 3s. 6d.

TAYLOR, Sir H.—**Works.** Complete in Five Volumes. Crown 8vo, 30s.

    Philip Van Artevelde. Fcap. 8vo, 3s. 6d.

    The Virgin Widow, etc. Fcap. 8vo, 3s. 6d.

    The Statesman. Fcap. 8vo, 3s. 6d.

TAYLOR, Augustus.—**Poems.** Fcap. 8vo, 5s.

Tennyson Birthday Book, The. Edited by EMILY SHAKESPEAR. 32mo, limp, 2s.; cloth extra, 3s.

    *** A superior Edition, printed in red and black, on antique paper, specially prepared. Small crown 8vo, extra, gilt leaves, 5s.; and in various calf and morocco bindings.

THORNTON, L. M.—**The Son of Shelomith.** Small crown 8vo, 3s. 6d.

TODHUNTER, Dr. J.—**Laurella,** and other Poems. Crown 8vo, 6s. 6d.

    Forest Songs. Small crown 8vo, 3s. 6d.

    The True Tragedy of Rienzi : a Drama. 3s. 6d.

    Alcestis : a Dramatic Poem. Extra fcap. 8vo, 5s.

WALTERS, Sophia Lydia.—**A Dreamer's Sketch Book.** With 21 Illustrations by Percival Skelton, R. P. Leitch, W. H. J. Boot, and T. R. Pritchett. Engraved by J. D. Cooper. Fcap. 4to, 12s. 6d.

WATTS, Alaric Alfred and Anna Mary Howitt.—**Aurora.** A Medley of Verse. Fcap. 8vo, bevelled boards, 5s.

WEBSTER, Augusta.—In a Day : a Drama. Small crown 8vo, 2s. 6d.
Disguises : a Drama. Small crown 8vo, 5s.
Wet Days. By a Farmer. Small crown 8vo, 6s.
WILLIAMS, J.—A Story of Three Years, and other Poems. Small crown 8vo, 3s. 6d.
Wordsworth Birthday Book, The. Edited by ADELAIDE and VIOLET WORDSWORTH. 32mo, limp cloth, 1s. 6d. ; cloth extra, 2s.
YOUNGS, Ella Sharpe.—Paphus, and other Poems. Small crown 8vo, 3s. 6d.

WORKS OF FICTION IN ONE VOLUME.

BANKS, Mrs. G. L.—God's Providence House. New Edition. Crown 8vo, 3s. 6d.
INGELOW, Jean.—Off the Skelligs : a Novel. With Frontispiece. Second Edition. Crown 8vo, 6s.
MACDONALD, G.—Castle Warlock. A Novel. New and Cheaper Edition. Crown 8vo, 6s.
Malcolm. With Portrait of the Author engraved on Steel. Sixth Edition. Crown 8vo, 6s.
The Marquis of Lossie. Fifth Edition. With Frontispiece. Crown 8vo, 6s.
St. George and St. Michael. Fourth Edition. With Frontispiece. Crown 8vo, 6s.
PALGRAVE, W. Gifford.—Hermann Agha : an Eastern Narrative. Third Edition. Crown 8vo, 6s.
SHAW, Flora L.—Castle Blair ; a Story of Youthful Days. New and Cheaper Edition. Crown 8vo, 3s. 6d.
STRETTON, Hesba.—Through a Needle's Eye : a Story. New and Cheaper Edition, with Frontispiece. Crown 8vo, 6s.
TAYLOR, Col. Meadows, C.S.I., M.R.I.A.—Seeta : a Novel. New and Cheaper Edition. With Frontispiece. Crown 8vo, 6s.
Tippoo Sultaun : a Tale of the Mysore War. New Edition, with Frontispiece. Crown 8vo, 6s.
Ralph Darnell. New and Cheaper Edition. With Frontispiece. Crown 8vo, 6s.
A Noble Queen. New and Cheaper Edition. With Frontispiece. Crown 8vo, 6s.
The Confessions of a Thug. Crown 8vo, 6s.
Tara : a Mahratta Tale. Crown 8vo, 6s.
Within Sound of the Sea. New and Cheaper Edition, with Frontispiece. Crown 8vo, 6s.

BOOKS FOR THE YOUNG.

Brave Men's Footsteps. A Book of Example and Anecdote for Young People. By the Editor of "Men who have Risen." With 4 Illustrations by C. Doyle. Eighth Edition. Crown 8vo, 3*s.* 6*d.*

COXHEAD, Ethel.—**Birds and Babies.** Imp. 16mo. With 33 Illustrations. Cloth gilt, 2*s.* 6*d.*

DAVIES, G. Christopher.—**Rambles and Adventures of our School Field Club.** With 4 Illustrations. New and Cheaper Edition. Crown 8vo, 3*s.* 6*d.*

EDMONDS, Herbert.—**Well Spent Lives :** a Series of Modern Biographies. New and Cheaper Edition. Crown 8vo, 3*s.* 6*d.*

EVANS, Mark.—**The Story of our Father's Love,** told to Children. Sixth and Cheaper Edition of Theology for Children. With 4 Illustrations. Fcap. 8vo, 1*s.* 6*d.*

JOHNSON, Virginia W.—**The Catskill Fairies.** Illustrated by Alfred Fredericks. 5*s.*

MAC KENNA, S. J.—**Plucky Fellows.** A Book for Boys. With 6 Illustrations. Fifth Edition. Crown 8vo, 3*s.* 6*d.*

REANEY, Mrs. G. S.—**Waking and Working ;** or, From Girlhood to Womanhood. New and Cheaper Edition. With a Frontispiece. Crown 8vo, 3*s.* 6*d.*

Blessing and Blessed : a Sketch of Girl Life. New and Cheaper Edition. Crown 8vo, 3*s.* 6*d.*

Rose Gurney's Discovery. A Book for Girls. Dedicated to their Mothers. Crown 8vo, 3*s.* 6*d.*

English Girls : Their Place and Power. With Preface by the Rev. R. W. Dale. Fourth Edition. Fcap. 8vo, 2*s.* 6*d.*

Just Anyone, and other Stories. Three Illustrations. Royal 16mo, 1*s.* 6*d.*

Sunbeam Willie, and other Stories. Three Illustrations. Royal 16mo, 1*s.* 6*d.*

Sunshine Jenny, and other Stories. Three Illustrations. Royal 16mo, 1*s.* 6*d.*

STOCKTON, Frank R.—**A Jolly Fellowship.** With 20 Illustrations. Crown 8vo, 5*s.*

STORR, Francis, and TURNER, Hawes.—**Canterbury Chimes ;** or, Chaucer Tales re-told to Children. With 6 Illustrations from the Ellesmere MS. Third Edition. Fcap. 8vo, 3*s.* 6*d.*

STRETTON, Hesba.—**David Lloyd's Last Will.** With 4 Illustrations. New Edition. Royal 16mo, 2*s.* 6*d.*

Tales from Ariosto Re-told for Children. By a Lady. With 3 Illustrations. Crown 8vo, 4*s.* 6*d.*

WHITAKER, Florence.—**Christy's Inheritance.** A London Story. Illustrated. Royal 16mo, 1*s.* 6*d.*

PRINTED BY WILLIAM CLOWES AND SONS, LIMITED, LONDON AND BECCLES.

www.ingramcontent.com/pod-product-compliance
Lightning Source LLC
Chambersburg PA
CBHW021110020726
47500CB00003B/695